A SELFISH HEART: A REGENCY ROMANCE

LANDON HOUSE (BOOK 2)

ROSE PEARSON

A SELFISH HEART

A REGENCY ROMANCE

Landon House

(Book 2)

By

Rose Pearson

A SELFISH HEART

"And so it is to be your turn, Lady Anna."

Anna clasped her hands tightly together at her heart, her excitement building as her lady's maid set the final touches to her hair.

"It is," she said softly, looking at her reflection and wondering if she would satisfy the *ton*. "Selina is, of course, also hoping for her success."

"Of course," the maid murmured, as Anna thought of her twin sister. Selina was a little quieter than she, certainly more reserved, and it seemed to Anna as though her sister would have to permit herself to be more forthcoming in both her speech and her character if she was to find any happiness. She, of course, had no such difficulty. Last Season had been her introduction to the *beau monde* and she had not had any particular difficulty with introductions, conversations, or dancing. In fact, she had relished every moment of it! It had not been for her to make a match, however, for her elder sister, Lady Rebecca, was to be the first. Much to Anna's delight,

Rebecca had managed to do so and was now happily wed and settled with her new husband.

How I hope I shall have just as much success this Season.

Sighing to herself, Anna smiled at her reflection, quite satisfied with her appearance. "You have done well," she said, rising swiftly. "Now, I must not be tardy." Turning to her lady's maid, she waited patiently for the final few finishing touches. She then turned to make her way below stairs, where she knew Lady Hayward would be waiting for her. Her hand tightened on the rail as she descended, afraid that she might tread on her new gown or make some other mishap that would cause her to be all the more tardy, but much to her relief, she had no difficulty at all. Taking a breath, she smoothed her skirts and, setting her shoulders, walked into the drawing-room.

The three within the room turned to look at her as one, with Lady Hayward's smile jumping instantly onto her face.

"My dear Lady Anna," she said, holding out both her hands to her. "How very good to see you again."

"And you, Lady Hayward," Anna replied, grasping the older woman's hands and thinking to herself that Lady Hayward had not aged in any way since she had last seen her. Her blue eyes were still bright, her smile broad, and her graying hair pulled back neatly. She wore a gown of dark blue, which, Anna had to admit, suited the lady very well.

"I am glad to be reacquainted with you," she answered as her sister drew closer to them, a gentle smile on her face. "I hope your family is well?"

Lady Hayward nodded. "Very well indeed, although most remain at home, of course. My eldest, Lord Hayward, has returned to London to continue under your father's guidance."

Anna nodded, recalling the agreement that had been made between her father, the Duke of Landon, and Lady Hayward. He was something of a neglectful father to his daughters—perhaps, in part, due to his lack of certainty as to how to raise such a brood! Last Season, he had clearly been uncertain about gowns and such things, only to meet Lady Hayward. An agreement had quickly struck up between them. Lady Hayward would assist the duke's daughters in their attempts to encourage not only the *right* kinds of suitors, but those that would treat them with kindness and appreciation. In return, her father would aid Lady Hayward's sons, the eldest of which had taken on the title. Things were going very well thus far, from what Anna understood, which gave her a good deal of hope regarding her own future.

"I am sure that you are eager to make your way to the ball," Lady Hayward said, evidently seeing the excitement in Anna's eyes. "And you, Lady Selina? Are you also anticipating your return to society?"

Anna looked to her sister, who was, much to her surprise, looking anxious.

"I confess I am a little apprehensive," Lady Selina admitted, even though Anna felt no such thing. "It seems so much more...important this Season."

"That is because it does hold more importance!" the Duke exclaimed, speaking for the first time. "You and your sister are to seek out suitable gentlemen so that your futures are settled and secure—much like Rebecca." He smiled fondly, reminding Anna that, despite her father's failings, he did care for them all very much indeed. "But have no fear, Selina," he continued, putting a hand on his daughter's shoulder. "Lady Hayward will guide you through the Season, just as she has done with Rebecca."

Lady Hayward seemed to glow at this remark, looking up at the duke with a calm, steady gaze. "I thank you for your belief in me, Your Grace," she said as Anna began to slowly back towards the door, her eagerness to depart growing so much that it felt as though she were being pulled there by an invisible thread. "I am certain that they will both do very well, indeed."

The Duke chuckled. "And if their endeavors come to naught, then they can try next Season," he said as Anna closed her eyes in frustration. How was she meant to begin such endeavors if they did not depart soon? It was all very well for Selina to feel such anxiety, but she did not, and there was no reason, therefore, for them to linger simply to reassure her sister! The best thing for Selina, Anna felt, was to make her way to the ball and begin to engage herself with society again. That was the only way to remove such anxiety.

"I think we should depart," Lady Hayward said with a twinkle in her eye. "Your sister appears to be making her way to the carriage already, Lady Selina!"

Her father fixed Anna with a hard stare, and Anna felt herself flush with embarrassment. She stopped walking backward, dropped her head, and clasped her hands in front of her, a little embarrassed that she had been reprimanded, albeit silently.

"I am sure all will be well," Lady Hayward said encouragingly, looping one arm through Lady Selina's and leading her towards the door. "Come now, Lady Selina. Let us go." With a warm smile towards Anna, she gestured for her to make her way to the door. Glancing at her father, Anna gave him a hurried smile and then turned to make her way out towards the front door and to the carriage. Despite the reprimand, her excitement grew steadily, and she found herself smiling as she climbed into the carriage.

It was the beginning of what she hoped would be an excellent and exciting Season, and Anna could hardly wait for it to begin.

"*I do* enjoy the first few weeks of the Season."

Elias grinned as he finished speaking, ignoring the dark look sent towards him by Lord Rowley.

"The only reason you appear to enjoy it, Lord Comerfield, is because you have the opportunity to make many new acquaintances," Lord Rowley replied, grimacing. "Acquaintances that you shall either choose to continue in the hope that they might..." Tilting his head, he considered for a moment. "That they might improve their acquaintance with you all the more. And, if you do not believe that they would be amicable to such an idea, then you bring the acquaintance to an end."

"And there can be nothing wrong with such actions!" Elias protested, still smiling broadly. "You know very well that I am always kind to those I consider debutantes and young ladies eager to wed. I never pursue them."

Lord Rowley arched one eyebrow, opened his mouth to make a response, only to close it again. With a heavy sigh, he shook his head and turned away, looking at the other guests and, no doubt, the many young ladies who were making either their first or second appearance in London.

"I do not think we should ever have become friends, had I a younger sister," Lord Rowley muttered, as Elias reached to take a glass of brandy, and then another one for Lord Rowley in an attempt to appease him.

"But you do not," Elias told him, shrugging. "And your elder sister is very happily wed, if I recall correctly."

"She is," Lord Rowley agreed, his dark look beginning to lift from his face. "Although if she was ever to be widowed, then that might be an entirely different matter!"

Elias chuckled. "I should never pursue your sister, Lord Rowley, truly. You have my word." He put his hand over his heart and bowed in a slightly mocking gesture. "Not when there are so many others here that might capture my attention!" The grin returned, but Lord Rowley ignored it, giving a small shake of his head and allowing a heavy sigh to escape from his lips as he surveyed the room. He and Elias had been friends for some time, and Elias knew that his friend was fully aware of the sort of gentleman he was. He was not yet called a 'rogue' by the *ton*, for he was not the sort to treat ladies with any sort of callous disregard, but certainly he had a reputation of being something of a flirt, of enjoying the company of beautiful, elegant, and genteel ladies—and if they were inclined towards him, then all the better! Elias was not going to deny that he had stolen kisses from some when the opportunity arose, but who could resist such a thing when it was practically handed to him? No, he enjoyed being a part of society and took as much from it as he could, despite the irritation and evident frustration of his friend.

"Then I suppose," Lord Rowley said, interrupting Elias' thoughts, "that this Season will be yet another where you give no consideration towards matrimony."

Elias let out a bark of laughter, throwing his head back as though Lord Rowley had said the most ridiculous of remarks.

"I shall take that to mean that you do not," Lord Rowley said dryly. "It might interest you to know, however, that what I have asked of you is precisely what I myself intend for this Season."

The smile faded from Elias' face as he looked at Lord Rowley steadily, trying to make out whether or not his friend was making a mockery of him. If he made any particular remark, then it might very well be that Lord Rowley, in turn, would laugh at *him* for believing such a thing.

"I am not pretending," Lord Rowley said wearily, passing one hand over his eyes. "You look at me as though I am gone quite mad, and I can assure you, I have not. I have, instead, given this a great deal of thought and considered it for many, many days. But I have come to the conclusion that now is the right and proper time for me to find a suitable young lady to wed. My family line must be continued, and the sooner I do such a thing, the better."

Elias did not know what to say to this, for he had never once heard Lord Rowley speak with such determination nor intent before. He had presumed, foolishly, it seemed, that he and Lord Rowley would continue through the London Season as they had these last few years—with nothing more than a vague interest in the ladies of the *beau monde* and enjoying the conversation and company of some. They might take note of the debutantes and might remark upon one or two in particular, but there was never any true interest in any of them. Never any suggestion that there might be more to an acquaintance that had first been intended.

It seemed now that such a thing was about to change and, for whatever reason, that sat uncomfortably upon Elias' shoulders.

"No doubt you will have some remark to make about how I am very foolish indeed," Lord Rowley sighed with a shake of his head. "You will laugh and say that there is no need for me to wed, that there must be something the matter with me to consider such a thing when I could enjoy the Season for what it is—but on this matter, I assure you, I will not be shaken." A steel glint entered his eye as his lips flattened, his jaw working for a moment. "And I shall not listen to any of your mockery either."

Elias held up one hand in a defensive manner, the other still holding his brandy. "I shall say nothing of the sort," he replied honestly. "I will confess to being a little surprised, but that is all I shall say." He was aware that his friend appeared determined about this decision and that to tease or to laugh would not do their friendship any good. Besides which, whilst he admitted that he was surprised at Lord Rowley's sudden intentions, he could not pretend that it was not wise. "You have more consideration and wisdom than I, Lord Rowley; that is for certain."

The glint left Lord Rowley's eyes as he looked back at Elias, clearly a little uncertain as to whether or not to believe him. Elias said nothing more but remained quite calm in his expression, being utterly truthful in his words.

"I will agree with that wholeheartedly," Lord Rowley replied after a few moments. "Although might such a decision on my part make you consider your own situation?" One eyebrow lifted, but Elias dismissed it with a swift shake of his head.

"Certainly not," he replied firmly. "You sound much like my dear mama, Lord Rowley. She has a way of suggesting that I might think of taking a wife without ever actually speaking those words!"

"You are the Marquess of Comerfield," Lord Rowley reminded him with a small lift of his brow. "It would be wise to take a wife and produce the heir."

With a sniff, Elias looked away. "I have an excellent younger brother who is already doing just as you have suggested," he stated firmly. "Should the worst happen— and I have no reason to believe that it will—then he will take the title. I cannot see any real need for haste when it comes to marriage."

"It is certainly true, then," Lord Rowley remarked in a dry tone. "True that I have a good deal more wisdom than you in this particular situation, it seems." He threw back the rest of his brandy and let out a sharp laugh, which, much to Elias' surprise, was a little cutting. "I shall not seek your advice when it comes to the ladies I consider, then."

Elias shrugged. "I do not see why I could not be of use," he replied, a little pained that his friend dismissed him so quickly. "Just because I have no intention of marriage does not mean that I am unable to give my opinion on a lady's character."

Lord Rowley considered this for a moment before, with a small sigh, shrugging in a most nonchalant manner. "If you wish to give me your thoughts, then I suppose I shall not refuse them," he said without any sort of eagerness.

"Then you have some particular ladies in mind?" Elias asked, but Lord Rowley quickly shook his head.

"I have only just returned to London and, unfortunately, none of the ladies I was acquainted with last Season hold any interest for me," he said with a slight shake of his head as though a little mournful about such a thing. "Therefore, I shall look at this year's debutantes and hope that one of them, at least, will be worthy of my consideration."

Elias lifted one eyebrow. "Might I remind you that you barely met any ladies of interest last Season, Lord Rowley," he replied, having a very clear memory of Lord Rowley and his particular behavior. "You were quite set upon enjoying the Season and tended to focus your time upon cards and dancing. That is hardly the setting to know a lady better, especially when one might be a little...overcome with the very best brandy that London has to offer." This, much to his delight, brought a look of embarrassment to Lord Rowley's face, although, after a moment, he began to nod.

"I suppose there is something to be said for that," he remarked, throwing Elias a hard look. "I shall not merely consider the debutantes, then."

"Capital!" Elias crowed, another grin spreading across his face. "For there are certainly one or two ladies I have in mind that might be more than suitable for you, Rowley."

His friend grimaced. "None that you have taken a particular interest in, I hope?"

"Precisely the opposite," Elias promised with a half bow. "Rather, they are ones who have refused me entirely. Thus, I am sure they are more than proper and would suit you very well, indeed."

For a few moments, Elias thought that his friend would refuse, that he would state that he had no need for such direction but, eventually, Lord Rowley sighed and nodded, evidently accepting Elias' help.

"Excellent!" Elias cried, turning his head so that he might look all around him. "Then there is no time to be wasted! Certainly, there is no need for us to stand here and watch all that goes on around us when there are so many ladies present this evening who might be very glad of your company!" Tilting his head, he looked all about him and took in a few ladies of his acquaintance that he knew Lord Rowley might consider. "Have you asked anyone to dance as yet?"

Lord Rowley shook his head.

"Then we must alter that at once!" Elias exclaimed, taking Lord Rowley's empty glass and handing it to a waiting footman. "Come now, we must enjoy ourselves this evening—and that begins with reacquainting ourselves with the lovely Lady Foster and her incorrigible daughter."

Lord Rowley's lip curled. "She is the most persistent

flirt," he complained, throwing him a suspicious look. "Are you quite certain that *she* is someone you wish me to consider?"

Elias laughed, shaking his head. "No, indeed not," he replied, "for both mother and daughter are much too improper in their manner and lack a great deal of decorum. No, rather, we shall reacquaint ourselves with them and, hopefully, have them introduce us to the other young ladies standing with them." His brow lifted as his friend's eyes caught sight of who he meant, thinking them very pretty young ladies indeed.

"Very well," Lord Rowley agreed after a few moments. "Let us hope that Miss Wilson does not immediately begin her flirtatious remarks, for I do not think I can manage much of a conversation if she persists in directing such statements and questions towards me!"

"I shall take them for you if I must," Elias replied, hiding his smile. He did not mind Miss Wilson's manner, managing to respond to her in much the same way but without ever intending to make any further commitment to her. "Come now, the evening is being wasted, and we have not taken one single dance as yet!" He chuckled and slapped Lord Rowley on the shoulder. "Mayhap we shall find your lady this very night! Mayhap she will stand before us, and you will think her so proper and perfect that your heart will sing with joy and you will cry out for her almost at once."

"I hardly think so," Lord Rowley replied, sighing heavily. "But I will be glad to make some new introductions, at least."

Elias shrugged and moved forward a little more,

aware of the moment Lady Foster and her daughter caught sight of them. His smile spread quickly at the flash of awareness in Lady Foster's eyes, as well as the faint blush that came into Miss Wilson's cheeks. This Season, it seemed, was going to be just as excellent and just as enjoyable as the last.

~

"AND SEE, I have returned you to your chaperone, just as I ought."

Miss Stirling looked up at Elias doubtfully, her expression still one of uncertainty and anxiousness. It had been clear from the very beginning that she had not wanted to dance with him, but her chaperone—a somewhat formidable aunt by the name of Lady Whitburn—had insisted that she do so. Elias had not found the dance enjoyable, for Miss Stirling had remained silent and pale throughout most of it as though afraid he might steal her away and never again return her to her aunt.

Elias had done as he knew was right, for whilst he might bear something of a reputation, it was not one that warned debutantes away from him. He had never toyed with nor ruined a young lady's reputation and had no intention of ever doing so. It seemed that Miss Stirling, however, did not believe such a thing, given just how fearfully she looked up at him.

"I do hope you enjoyed the dance, Miss Stirling," he said with a respectful bow. "I found it to be most pleasing." This was a lie, of course, but it was not as though he could state the truth. Miss Stirling nodded and mumbled something under her breath, earning her a hard glare from her aunt, which then resulted in her thanking Elias properly.

"You are most welcome," he said, deciding that he ought to take his leave and thinking quietly that he would not recommend Miss Stirling to Lord Rowley. He could not have his friend wed such a creature, not when it might put enmity between them both!

"Oh, Lord Comerfield!" Lady Whitburn exclaimed, her eyes going to someone over Elias' shoulder. "I should make an introduction, if you will permit it?"

A little surprised, Elias nodded and looked over his shoulder, making certain to step out of the way so that the lady in question could come forward and greet Lady Whitburn warmly, obviously very glad to see her again.

"You have *two* this year, do you not?" Lady Whitburn asked the lady, who nodded. "My goodness, such a responsibility!"

"But a very satisfactory one, I assure you," came the reply as the lady turned to face Elias. "The duke is helping my son with some complicated business matters that require his attention, and I am truly grateful to him for doing so."

Lady Whitburn nodded sagely. "But of course," she said quietly. "And now, might I introduce the Marquess of Comerfield?" She gestured towards him. "Lord Comerfield, Lady Hayward."

Confused as to why Lady Whitburn had been so very eager to introduce him to a lady who appeared to be much older than he himself, Elias nonetheless bowed in greeting and murmured a few words of welcome.

"How very good to meet you," Lady Hayward replied as she rose from her curtsy. "Lady Whitburn and I are old friends. How strange it is now to be in London with our charges when I remember our own days in the London Season as though it were only yesterday!"

Elias smiled politely. "You have charges of your own, Lady Hayward?" he asked, only for the lady to take a small step forward and beckon towards someone behind Elias.

"Yes, yes, I do," she replied quickly. "Lady Whitburn is very kind to think of them. This is our first ball of the Season, you understand."

Another quick smile crossed Elias' face as he waited for this particular young lady to reach him, not quite certain that Lady Whitburn knew of his reputation if she was so willing to have young ladies introduced to him in such a manner!

"This is Lady Selina," Lady Hayward said warmly. "And her twin sister, Lady Anna."

Surprise filled Elias as he turned his head, watching the two young ladies drawing near to Lady Hayward. For twins, there were certainly similarities but nothing of particular note. One had brown hair with eyes flecked with green and brown, whilst the other had lighter hair than the first and, as he looked into her eyes, saw that they were much deal greener than her sisters.

"Twins?" he remarked, before realizing that he had not bowed, nor greeted them properly. A little embarrassed, he did so at once as Lady Hayward quickly introduced him to her charges. The two young ladies sank into beautiful, elegant curtsies, and, by the time they rose, the embarrassment had faded from Elias.

"Yes, we are twins, Lord Comerfield," said the first, her curls appearing a little bronzed in the candlelight, making him think her pretty. "Although it appears we are not as similar as some might anticipate!"

"There are certainly similarities between you both," he said, wondering if she had known what he had been thinking, "and I could certainly tell that you were sisters."

The young lady—the one he thought to be Lady Anna—laughed lightly, whilst the other remained silent but managed a small smile, her eyes drifting away from him in a disinterested manner. Elias felt himself a little frustrated at this but kept his attention upon Lady Anna.

"And you are enjoying the Season?" he asked, only to remember that Lady Hayward had stated that this was their first ball of the Season.

Lady Anna was quick to remind him.

"This is only our first outing in London, Lord Comerfield," she answered, "although it is certainly an excellent one. I had forgotten quite what joy such an outing can bring!"

His brows rose. They were not debutantes, then, as he had assumed.

"Lady Anna and Lady Selina were in London last Season," Lady Hayward told him as though she could see his thoughts. "Their eldest sister, Lady Rebecca, soon became engaged to Lord Richmond. They are now quite settled in his country estate."

Elias' brow lifted. He recalled something of a scandal last Season to do with Lord Richmond, although the details of it, he could not quite remember. "I see," he replied, understanding at once. It was always most important to have the eldest daughter wed and settled first, before the younger sisters had their opportunity. It seemed, however, that both Lady Anna and Lady Selina were now being given such an opportunity—and at once, Elias' thoughts turned to Lord Rowley. It would be an excellent thing to have him introduced to two such ladies, for whilst Lady Selina was quiet, Lady Anna was not, and he might take to one of them.

"Might I ask if you have any dances remaining, Lady Anna?" he asked, with a small inclination of his head. "Lady Selina? I should be very glad to dance with you both if you have the opportunity?"

Lady Anna smiled at him and slipped off her dance card at once, whilst Lady Selina took a few moments and a glance towards her chaperone before she did so. Satisfied, Elias wrote his name for first the country dance with Lady Anna and then the quadrille for Lady Selina. Hopefully, by the end of the evening, he would have found an opportunity to introduce both to Lord Rowley.

"I look forward to dancing with you both later," he said, handing the cards back to the ladies. "And now, I must excuse myself, for Miss Arbuckle will be waiting for me for the cotillion."

The two ladies smiled and nodded as Elias took his leave, and Elias departed their company with a broad smile on his face. Lord Rowley would not be able to state that Elias was doing nothing to assist him in his desire to find a suitable lady to wed, not when he had found two such ladies already! Lady Anna, he considered, making his way towards Miss Arbuckle, was certainly more engaging than her sister, and it was for that reason alone that Elias thought to recommend her a little more strongly than the first.

Whilst I continue enjoying the Season for what it is, he told himself, his smile spreading across his face as he made his way across the ballroom floor. *And that, certainly, will be more than enough for me.*

CHAPTER TWO

Anna sat back in her chair and let out a long breath, finding, much to her surprise, that she was fatigued after an afternoon spent greeting, conversing, and drinking tea with the many gentlemen that had come to call. She should be very grateful for their company, she knew, but it certainly would take her a little time to become used to such a thing!

"Well!" Lady Hayward exclaimed, smiling brightly at Anna before turning to Lady Selina. "That went very well, indeed."

"I am very glad to hear you say so," Anna replied with a smile. "There were certainly many gentlemen, more than I expected!"

"Which is all the better," Lady Hayward replied with a twinkle in her eye. "Now, did any such gentlemen spark any particular interest, Lady Anna?" She held Anna's gaze for a moment before looking to Lady Selina. "And you, Lady Selina?"

Anna shook her head, speaking honestly. "They were

all very genteel, certainly, and I should be glad to speak to them again," she replied, a touch embarrassed to be speaking so openly but knowing that she needed to do so should she have a successful Season. "I could not say that any caught my interest, but then again, Lady Hayward, I do not know them very well at all."

Lady Hayward smiled and nodded. "A very considered response," she said, making Anna flush with satisfaction. "It will be with both of you as it was with your sister. I shall guide you, of course, but my advice will be to seek out and settle upon a gentleman who is not only entirely suitable for you in terms of title, situation, and fortune, but also one who intrigues you." Her smile softened. "It is best, I believe, for a contented marriage to find a husband whose company you not only enjoy but feel as though you cannot do without—and likewise, for him also. That will bring about happiness for you, I am sure of it."

Anna tipped her head thoughtfully. "I have always thought Rebecca did very well for herself," she said slowly. "I know, however, that there were a few concerns about Lord Richmond." Her gaze fixed to Lady Hayward. "You did not dissuade her?"

"I did," Lady Hayward replied with a small smile. "Initially, certainly. But your sister proved that her belief in Lord Richmond was not misplaced and, should you ask her, she will tell you that she cannot explain the reason that she was drawn to him so but that such a feeling still remains, even though she is wed. *That* is what I would hope for you both. It is what I would encourage you to consider at length and, instead of merely settling for someone who is suitable, choose a gentleman who has captured your affections."

A tightness suddenly came into Anna's chest and she looked away from Lady Hayward, a small frown flickering across her brow. Her affections? She was not certain that such a thing could ever really be, given she had never experienced such a thing before. Yes, there had been flickers of interest in certain gentlemen last Season, but she had never once found herself captivated by any of them. Was it possible that such a thing might occur? She could tell from the way Rebecca and her new husband had simply *looked* at each other on their wedding day that there had been a great deal of affection between them, but she had considered it to be something that came with time and, perhaps, was only for the very few rather than for her herself. Her father, even though he had spoken very little to her about her future and the like, had always stated, quite plainly, that he expected them all to marry *suitable* gentleman—and by that, he meant that they would have a high title, an excellent fortune, and an exceptional family line. That had always been what Anna had considered to be of the greatest importance and she had never truly considered her own feelings on the matter. Yes, she would certainly expect to like her husband, but to have any more feelings than that was quite unfamiliar to her.

"You look troubled, Lady Anna."

Anna jerked her head back towards Lady Hayward, smiling at her quickly. "No, no," she replied hastily. "I am quite all right. It was only that I was thinking about the gentlemen that called this afternoon." She waved a hand airily, hiding her true thoughts from her chaperone. "I felt no particular interest towards any of them, as I have said. Does that mean that I should give them no further consideration?"

Lady Hayward contemplated for a moment, then shook her head. "Interest can be immediate, or it can grow over time," she replied quietly as Lady Selina reached to finish her cup of tea. "You were wise in what you said previously, Lady Anna. Do not permit my words to confuse you."

Satisfied that she had managed to convince Lady Hayward of such a thing, Anna sat back in her chair and thanked her, seeing Lady Hayward smile.

"Now, are we to make for the fashionable hour?" Lady Hayward asked, rising from her chair. "If we are, then you have time to make certain that you are quite prepared before we must depart."

Anna, who well remembered the times she had enjoyed in Hyde Park the previous Season, rose at once.

"Yes, certainly!" she exclaimed, wondering if she might change her gown for fear that the gentlemen who had called upon her this afternoon might also be present in Hyde Park and would see her in the same attire. "I am sure I have one or two curls that need to be pinned again." She hurried to the door, with her sister following suit as Lady Hayward herself remained sitting in her chair.

"I shall finish my tea and await your return," Lady Hayward said with a smile. "Take as much time as you need, Lady Anna, Lady Selina. The *ton* awaits!"

~

Hyde Park was much busier than Anna remembered. Whether it was the fact that she had been absent from London for some months or whether it was, in fact, a little busier than she recalled, she could not quite say. But the excitement that filled her as she descended from the carriage was very much the same as she had felt last Season, for her heart was thunderous with anticipation and her eyes darting from place to place as she looked all about her.

"Is this not quite wonderful, Selina?" she breathed as her sister came to stand beside her. "To be seen in such a way and to be of note to others is..." She could not express herself completely, her hands clasping tightly together as she let out a very contented sigh. "There is no need for us to allow another to the fore, as we had to do last Season with Rebecca. Now, it is to be our turn to step forward and to present ourselves to the *beau monde!*"

Lady Selina smiled and nodded, although she did not appear to be as excited as Anna had expected. But, then again, Lady Selina had always been a good deal more reserved than she and did not express the truth of her emotions as easily as Anna did.

"Look, there is Lord Stevenson!" Anna exclaimed, although a sharp look from Lady Hayward had her lowering her voice at once. "And he is speaking with Lord Comerfield." Her gaze shot to her sister who did not, however, express any delight at such a thing. "I do not know the third gentleman, however."

"Then why do we not go and speak to them all?"

Lady Hayward suggested, clearly aware that Anna was eager to enter into conversation with them. "Come now, let us walk together and I am sure that either Lord Comerfield or Lord Stevenson will greet us."

Anna stepped forward confidently, her head held high as she walked alongside her sister. She knew that she looked well, for her brown curls were held neatly under her bonnet, with only a few escaping to brush alongside her temples. Having changed into another gown, which had met with Lady Hayward's approval for the colors suited her very well, indeed, Anna felt quite contented with her appearance, which only added to her self-assurance.

"Good afternoon, Lady Hayward, Lady Anna, Lady Selina!"

It was not Lord Comerfield that spoke first but rather Lord Stevenson, who, upon catching sight of them, turned his head and stepped to one side so that they might immediately be welcomed into his conversation. Anna curtsied and smiled prettily, for Lord Stevenson was a handsome gentleman, even if his title was only that of a viscount.

"Good afternoon," she murmured, glancing towards Lord Comerfield and noting how he was studying her, his gaze roving from the top of her head to her toes. It was only when he looked back into her face that he realized she had been watching him and, despite the flush of heat that coursed through her, betraying her obvious embarrassment, Lord Comerfield grinned.

A twist of dislike entered Anna's heart. Lord Comerfield was plainly aware that he was a very handsome gentleman indeed, with dark brown eyes that whispered of a few too many secrets whenever he looked at her and a smile that she was sure had captured the heart of many a lady. There was a boyishness to his features, perhaps in the way that his brown hair flopped across his forehead, or in the way that his lips tipped in a lop-sided smile. Regardless of that, however, Anna felt no inclination towards him, thinking him to be something of a rascal in the way that he conducted himself. She had found him to be pleasant enough at the ball last evening, and he had danced very well indeed, but she had been fully aware of just how often his eyes had strayed towards the other ladies in their set, rather than concentrating on her and her alone.

It was to be expected, she supposed, but certainly, he was not someone that she would ever consider further.

"How glad I am that you have joined us this after-noon!" Lord Comerfield exclaimed, turning his attention to Lady Hayward. "Last evening, I wanted very much to introduce your charges to my dear friend Lord Rowley, but found myself quite unable to do so, given that Lady Anna and Lady Selina were both already quite busy with their many, many dances." He smiled warmly, but Anna did not return it, her gaze settling on the gentleman she was not yet acquainted with. "Might I have opportunity to do so now?"

Lady Hayward inclined her head. "But of course."

"Then might I introduce the Earl of Rowley," he continued, gesturing to his friend who bowed hastily, clearly a little surprised at the swiftness of such introduc-tions. "Lord Rowley, this is Lady Anna and Lady Selina, daughters both to the Duke of Landon. And, of course, Lady Hayward, who is their chaperone at present."

Lord Rowley cleared his throat gently before greeting them all in turn, clearly identifying which of them was Lady Anna and which was Lady Selina by the conversation that had taken place thus far. Anna smiled brightly back at him whilst Selina kept her gaze low and her smile demure.

"Good afternoon, Lord Rowley," she replied, leaving her sister standing mutely beside her. "I am glad to make your acquaintance. Have you been in London for long?"

Lord Rowley was a handsome gentleman, with dark hair and blue eyes, firm shoulders, and a strong back. His hands were clasped behind him, puffing his chest out just a little and making her in mind of a bird that was very proud of its plumage.

"I have been here for a little over a fortnight," he told her, a small smile lifting only one side of his mouth. "You have only just arrived, I understand?"

She nodded, wondering whether or not this meant that he and Lord Comerfield had discussed her and her sister. "Indeed," she answered quietly. "Our first ball was only last evening."

"And I was very sorry not to make your acquaintance there," he said with a small inclination of his head as though he was truly apologetic. "Perhaps at the next ball, you might permit me a dance?"

A small flush caught her cheeks as she accepted such a request, a little surprised that he appeared so eager when they had only just become acquainted.

"And you also, Lady Selina," he continued, turning to

her sister and flooding Anna with a mixture of disappointment and embarrassment as she realized Lord Rowley was being nothing more than gentlemanlike in his compliments and his requests. A little ashamed of her own high opinion, she did not say much more, remaining silent until Lord Comerfield spoke to her directly.

"Tell me, Lady Anna, what do you think of London thus far?"

"I hardly know," she answered, one eyebrow lifting just a little. "I have only been here for a short time and my memories of last Season are a little dulled by time."

He laughed, and Anna's gaze slid towards her sister, noting how she was still conversing with Lord Rowley whilst Lady Hayward watched on approvingly, speaking herself to Lord Stevenson, who, thus far, had shown no particular interest in either sister.

"But you were present in London last Season, from what I understand?" he said, as she nodded. "There must be some parts of society that still bring a thrill of excitement to your heart?"

She did not much like his question, finding it a trifle too probing for someone who had only just become a new acquaintance. "I enjoy balls, certainly," she said, not willing to say much more. "But I also find a great deal to enjoy when it comes to the more regular activities, such as taking tea at Gunter's or walking through the park when the sun is shining and the air is warm."

His brows lifted, although the smile that crossed his face was one that held just a hint of mockery. "Very poetic, Lady Anna," he said, although the remark brought no smile to her face. "I confess that I am much more inclined towards the great, exciting events of the Season! I find very little enjoyment in the quieter activities."

"Such as walking in Hyde Park and quietly conversing?" Anna interrupted before she could stop herself. It was a brazen remark, she was aware, but there was something about Lord Comerfield that she was beginning to dislike intensely. To suggest that he found a lack of enjoyment in the very activity they were engaging in at present was not only rude, but highly disrespectful, and Anna did not mind one bit to see the astonishment jump into his expression.

Lord Comerfield stared at her for some moments before a hard laugh left him, and he looked at her as though he had never quite seen her before.

"Indeed, you are quite right to reprimand me, Lady Anna," he said as Lady Selina let out a quiet laugh beside her, frustrating Anna all the more that her sister appeared to be having an excellent conversation whilst she struggled with Lord Comerfield. "But what I shall say, in the hope of pleasing you, is that the conversation *we* share, at present, is not at all dull nor staid. In fact, I have quite enjoyed myself thus far."

Anna did not smile at him, her gaze steady and her resolve firm. "Then you speak only for yourself, Lord Comerfield," she answered, tightly. "For it seems that I cannot say the same."

This, it seemed, surprised him so much that, for a short time, he was unable to even make a response. His eyes were fixed to hers, his mouth a little ajar and a spark of astonishment in his gaze as he looked at her. Anna said nothing more, turning herself bodily towards

Lord Rowley and her sister, glad indeed to put such a conversation to bed. She did not want to speak to Lord Comerfield any further and would have been glad to remove herself from his presence at once, had it not been for the fact that Lady Selina and Lady Hayward were still deep in conversation with the other two gentlemen.

"Then I should be glad to send you all an invitation," Lord Stevenson declared, as Lady Hayward laughed and thanked him. "For what is a dinner party without an excellent number of wonderful guests?"

"You are very kind," Lady Hayward said, throwing a quick glance towards Anna and Selina. "Ladies, Lord Stevenson has, only just now, invited us to his dinner party next week. I believe an invitation will be sent very soon."

This, at least, made Anna smile. "How wonderful!" she exclaimed as Lord Stevenson inclined his head with evident satisfaction that had secured their interest. "I thank you, Lord Stevenson."

"As do I," Lady Selina added quickly. "That is very kind of you, Lord Stevenson."

The gentleman let out a chuckle and shook his head. "It will be my pleasure to have you all," he replied with an inclination of his head. "Your father will be invited also, and I must hope that he shall attend, for it will be a very great honor!"

At this, Lady Hayward made to take their leave and, with a curt nod towards Lord Comerfield, a murmur of farewell to Lord Rowley and one final expression of thanks to Lord Stevenson, Anna made her way across the park a little more, walking between her sister and Lady Hayward.

"Well?" Lady Hayward asked the moment they had removed themselves from the gentlemen. "What was the conversation like?"

Much to Anna's surprise, Lady Selina smiled brightly. "Lord Rowley has excellent conversation," she replied, appearing more animated than Anna had seen her in some days. "I very much enjoyed speaking with him. And Lord Stevenson is very kind to invite us all!"

Lady Hayward laughed softly, although she raised a hand to wave one warning finger in the air. "You must be careful of Lord Stevenson," she said carefully. "I have known him for some time, for he is the son of a dear acquaintance of mine, and his interest will not be in you yourselves, my dear ladies, but rather in the increase such a connection can bring to him."

Anna frowned. "What do you mean?"

"She means," Lady Selina said before Lady Hayward could explain, "that Lord Stevenson is more interested in having a connection to the dukedom rather than to have any true interest in either one of us."

There came no disappointment with such a state-ment but rather an understanding that there were such gentlemen within society and that, as such, a warning from Lady Hayward was much appreciated.

"I see," Anna replied with a small shrug. "Then, while I shall be very glad indeed for his invitation and his company, I shall not give the gentleman himself much consideration!"

Lady Hayward chuckled. "A very wise idea, Lady

Anna," she said, looking at her. "And Lord Comerfield? How was his conversation?"

Anna hesitated, the smile fading from her expression. "I found him much too forward and a little rude," she answered quietly. "I do not think he has excellent conversation or any such thing, such as Lady Selina found with Lord Rowley."

Lady Hayward nodded slowly, making sure to keep her voice slow so that she was not overheard. "Then I would rely on your own judgment at present and remain less than well acquainted with him," she answered. "I do not know anything about the marquess, save for the fact that he holds an excellent title and is often found in society seeking to make himself acquainted with as many young ladies as possible!" Her smile was rueful. "There may be more to his character than that, of course, but I believe your awareness of his conversation speaks of it well thus far."

Anna tossed her head. "I have no intention of improving my acquaintance with Lord Comerfield," she answered firmly. "And, Selina, I do not think that you should do so either."

Lady Selina frowned. "I am able to make my own decisions, Anna," she retorted, a hint of irritation in her voice. "It might be that I find his conversation very different from what you yourself experienced. No, I shall not choose to follow in your footsteps but fully intend to discover the truth of it for myself."

Anna looked towards Lady Hayward, expecting her to say something but, much to her surprise, the lady remained silent. It irritated her somewhat that her sister would not simply listen to what she herself had experienced rather than stubbornly refusing to do so and, instead, being quite determined to make up her own mind on certain matters. But seeing that Lady Hayward was not about to say anything in agreement with this, Anna lapsed into a frustrated silence.

"Ah, now, here is Lady Tollsworth and her two daughters," Lady Hayward said after a few moments. "They will make excellent acquaintances for you, I am sure."

And thus, Anna was forced to set her irritations aside and, instead, to put a smile on her face and permit Lady Hayward to introduce her to three new acquaintances. Hyde Park, so far, was not all that Anna had expected and she found herself a trifle disillusioned. Lord Comerfield, she considered, was rather to blame for such a thing, and she could only hope that any other gentlemen they met this afternoon would have better conversation and better manners than he! Else she feared she would return home most disappointed, and that was the last thing Anna wanted!

CHAPTER THREE

O*ne week later*

"AND THUS, it seems, your quest for a suitable bride is still ongoing!"

"Yes," Lord Rowley replied with a hint of irritation in his voice. "I am well aware of that, Lord Comerfield."

Elias chuckled and looked about the room as he accepted a glass of brandy from one of the waiting footmen. "Well, Lord Stevenson's dinner party might well be the opportunity you require to satisfy yourself that either Lady Anna or Lady Selina could suit you," he said, as Lord Rowley narrowed his eyes. "Or there is Miss Whitburn? I believe she is here this evening. And then Lady Robertson, who—whilst widowed—is still young enough to wed!"

"To the latter, I shall refuse," Lord Rowley replied with a grimace. "I am very well aware that Lady

Robertson is not only a widow, but a wealthy one at that. I have no belief that she has any eagerness towards matrimony whatsoever." He eyed Elias speculatively. "Besides which, I am sure that she is one of your *many* acquaintances who has behaved warmly towards you in the past, is that not so?"

Elias did not immediately respond, having no wish to tell Lord Rowley that what he said was quite true, nor indeed that he hoped that such an opportunity might present itself to him again. Instead, he cleared his throat and shrugged. "Lady Robertson does look very similar to both Lady Anna and Lady Selina, in her own way," he said, ignoring Lord Rowley's snort of disapproval. "She has the same brown hair and is of the same height."

"But aside from that is very different indeed," Lord Rowley replied, evidently realizing that Elias was struggling to find anything to say that would remove the need to answer his question. "There is nothing similar about them at all, save for that they are of equal height and bear the same shade in their hair. You are merely trying to distract me from my remark so that you will not have to confirm it to me, but, in doing so, you have confirmed it to me already."

Shrugging, Elias made to say something more, only for the bell to ring for dinner. Grinning at his escape, he made his way towards the assembling line, ready to lead through whichever lady was to be his. With the smile still on his face, he made his way to the dining room, leading one Lady Chesterton with him, who seemed to think his smile was for her alone. Within minutes, they were all seated around the table, and Elias could not help but notice how quickly Lord Rowley began a conversation with Miss Whittaker, who was next to him. Lord Rowley did not even glance up for, if he had, Elias was quite certain that his friend would have reacted to the sight of Lady Robertson sitting down next to Elias, although he was quite delighted at the company. It seemed that all mention of Lady Robertson was, for the time being at least, quite forgotten.

"You appear to be very pleased indeed with the dinner party this evening, Lord Comerfield," Lady Robertson murmured as the first course was served to them. "Or is it the company you have by you that makes you smile so?"

Elias could not help but chuckle, looking at the lady with a lifted brow. "I should not like to say, Lady Robertson, for fear of offending or complimenting you," he answered, making her smile back at him. "I should not like to be accused of either!" One small glance to his left showed him that Lady Chesterton was paying no attention to the conversation he was having with Lady Robertson, seemingly quite taken up with Lord Crawley, who was on her other side. "And what do you say, Lady Robertson? Are you pleased with this evening's company?"

"How could I not be?" she asked with a teasing smile. "I have only just returned to London and now I find myself surrounded by those I consider to be the very best of my acquaintances!"

"I shall take that as a very warm compliment, indeed, Lady Robertson," he replied, surprised at how his heart quickened. "You are much too kind."

She smiled at him but said nothing more, turning back to her meal and beginning to eat. Elias followed suit, although he found himself pleased with all that had been said thus far between himself and the lady. There had only been a few moments with Lady Robertson last Season, moments when she had stepped into his arms and he had found himself lost in her presence, only for her to pull away again and laugh, dancing away from him as though she was always to be out of his reach, always to be pursued. He knew full well that she had no intention of marrying at present, which, to his mind, had made her all the more attractive to him. Was there a suggestion that things might continue on as they had begun?

Or does she now seek a husband?

The thought dashed the smile from his face in a moment. He did not want to consider such a thing as yet and, whilst Lady Robertson's overtures towards him were welcome, he did not want them to mean anything more than what they were at present.

By the time the ladies left the table, Elias found himself in a much better mood. The excellent food, the plentiful wine, and the wonderful conversation had lightened his spirits and chased away any dark thoughts that he had been considering regarding Lady Robertson. She had murmured more than a few things to him, and he had found himself delighting in her company all the more. The suggestion that there might be more to their acquaintance than before brought him both hope and anticipation, which he found more and more difficult to contain.

"Port!" Lord Stevenson cried as the footmen began to set it out for each gentleman present. "This has been an excellent evening and I cannot thank you enough for your company!" He raised his glass. "A toast!"

More than willing, Elias picked up his glass and held it high. The gentlemen toasted themselves—their own fine company—before he took a mouthful. The sweet liquor ran down his throat and into his chest, warming him, and he chuckled loudly as Lord Stevenson instructed the footmen to pour them all a little more. Knowing that he was to sit with the ladies for the remainder of the evening, Elias was determined not to lose himself in his cups, but he had to admit that the port was very fine indeed.

When the time came for the gentlemen to make their way through to the ladies, Elias found it a little more diffi-cult than usual to rise from the table without swaying. Frustrated at himself for drinking more than he had meant, he took a firm grip of his chair and lowered his head.

"I will join you in a few minutes," he managed to say as a bark of laughter from another gentleman shot through his head, perhaps laughing at the state of him. Flushed with embarrassment, he waved a hand. "Forgive me."

"Not at all," Lord Stevenson chuckled as the other gentlemen began to file out of the room. "Do ask the footmen for anything you might need."

Elias nodded and took a deep breath, his hands still gripping the back of his chair as mortification flooded him. He had not meant to make such a fool of himself, and yet, despite the knowledge of his idiocy, he found himself overcome with an insatiable urge to laugh. And so, laugh he did, the sound echoing around the room as he thought of just how foolish he must now appear to the other gentlemen. He certainly could not join the ladies in such a state as this!

"Water," he muttered, one of the footmen hurrying off at once in order to fetch him what he required. His laughter subsiding, he sat back down in his chair and waited for the servant to return. His stomach twisted for a moment and he closed his eyes, desperate not to allow any feelings of illness to overcome him.

"My lord?"

Opening his eyes, Elias accepted the water from the footman and proceeded to drink it slowly, so that he would not make himself feel even worse! Thankfully, after a few minutes, he was able to stand without difficulty and, all the better, make his way to the door. His head had cleared somewhat and he was no longer afraid that he would behave in an idiotic manner in front of the other guests.

Walking through the door and along the hallway to the drawing-room, Elias stopped suddenly. A figure had emerged from a small room to his left and, having evidently not seen him, was now making her way back towards the drawing-room. His brows rose. In the candle-light, he was certain that the lady in question was none other than Lady Robertson.

"You have not been searching for me, I hope?" he murmured, hearing the swift intake of breath that came from her as he hurried towards her, his hands grasping her shoulders lightly. "In fact, no—I *do* hope, in fact, that you have been searching for me. Our conversation has filled me with great anticipation."

The lady said nothing, her silence encouraging him all the more. Was she waiting for him to act? To prove to her that he was just as eager for her acquaintance this Season as he had been the last? Boldly, he dropped his head and pressed his cheek to hers, one hand now resting on her waist. "I will prove my eagerness for your affections, if I must."

"Please!"

The word was a strangled squeak but, before he could step back, a loud exclamation came from behind him. Turning, he dropped his hands from the lady before him and realized, with shock and utter dread, that it was *not* Lady Robertson whom he had been cradling. The lady in question turned slowly to face him, her eyes wide with evident fear, her mouth slack with the evident horror of what he had done.

"Unhand that young lady at once, Lord Comerfield!"

Lady Chesterton strode towards him, her face bright red with evident shock and dismay. "Whatever do you think you are doing?"

Elias held up both hands in defense. "Forgive me," he said haltingly. "I—I did not mean to..." He slowly realized that the young lady, who now had both hands clutched in front of her and her eyes wide and fixed to his with fear, was none other than Lady Anna.

Lady Anna, his mind screamed. *The daughter of a duke!*

"Please," he said, again, as Lady Chesterton wrapped

one arm around Lady Anna's shoulders. "I thought her someone else. That is all."

"And is this the sort of thing you do to young ladies who are merely making their way back from the retiring room?" Lady Chesterton demanded, her voice so loud that it seemed to boom across the hallway. Elias closed his eyes, knowing that he could not ask her to quieten her voice but afraid that, if she did not, the rest of the guests would hear her and might come to investigate.

His fears, it seemed, were to be proven correct.

"I did not mean to behave so towards you, Lady Anna," he said hastily, "I thought you to be another of my acquaintances, one who has..." He could not bring himself to finish the question, his horror increasing all the more as the drawing-room door opened and Lord Stevenson himself stepped out.

"Is something the matter?" he asked as Lady Chesterton turned both herself and Lady Anna around. "What has occurred?"

"You might well ask, Lord Stevenson!" Lady Chesterton exclaimed, her voice still overly loud. "I came upon this gentleman attempting to embrace poor Lady Anna, who was quite terrified and unable to remove herself from his grasp!"

"I am quite all right," Lady Anna replied, her voice shaking just a little as Lord Stevenson came further towards them all. "It was a misunderstanding, that is all."

Lord Stevenson frowned darkly. "A misunderstanding?" he replied, just as Lady Hayward came out of the drawing-room and made her way swiftly to her charge, who stepped away from Lady Chesterton at once.

"I thought her to be someone else," Elias replied heavily, certain now that all of the guests present would have heard what had happened. "In truth, I did not believe it to be Lady Anna." His head began to grow fuzzy and he pressed one hand to it, wincing as he did so. Lord Stevenson, however, did not appear to have any sympathy whatsoever, for his expression was tight with anger.

"You mean to say that you placed your hands upon a young lady?" Lord Stevenson demanded as Lady Anna finally turned her head to look at him, her own eyes welling up with tears.

"I did," Elias answered, choosing to be honest and accept whatever consequence came to him rather than pretending otherwise. "As I have said, I believed her to be someone else entirely. It was a mistake, and I can only beg her forgiveness." He inclined his head towards Lady Anna, not missing the fury that had etched itself onto Lady Hayward's face as she looked back at him. Shame covered him from head to foot, and he hung his head, knowing that he deserved every bit of anger and upset that came towards him.

"We should take you back to the other guests," he heard Lady Hayward say, clearly determined that she should ignore his request for an apology. "It may be that you can remove yourself from this quite quickly, Lady Anna."

His head lifted, his heart beginning to pound furiously in his chest. "It was a mistake on my part," he found himself saying, weakly. "There can be no stain on Lady Anna's reputation."

Lady Chesterton laughed harshly. "You may say so, Lord Comerfield, but we must leave that up to the *ton* to decide," she told him sternly. "What you have done could have severe consequences."

Elias swallowed his retort and did not say a word in response, even though in his heart, he felt a swirl of anger towards Lady Chesterton. If she had only remained quiet, had spoken with a little more decorum, then mayhap Lord Stevenson would not have overheard them and been required to step out into the hallway. All might have been easily set aside, rather than the current difficulty that he now found himself in.

Do not blame others for what you yourself have done.

Taking in a deep breath, Elias lifted his chin and looked towards Lady Anna, hating the tears that were still glistening in her eyes and feeling a great shame wash over him once more.

"I will do whatever I can to help you, Lady Anna," he said slowly, knowing that there might well be an expectation upon him to do a little more than merely aid her, but knowing in his heart that he would never willingly marry the lady to save her reputation, even if it *was* his doing. "This has been a very grave mistake, and, as I have said, I can only apologize."

"Let us hope it is not as you fear, Lady Chesterton," Lady Hayward remarked, her arm still around Lady Anna's shoulders. "We need not say anything more to anyone else within the house at present." Her eyes fixed to Lord Stevenson. "What say you, Lord Stevenson?"

The gentleman stared for a moment, then nodded his head fervently. "I have no wish to damage Lady Anna's reputation, not when it was so clearly an accident," he said, shooting a furious glance toward Elias. "of course, there is no need to make mention of it to anyone."

"Good," Lady Hayward replied, not looking at Elias at all. "Then allow me to take Lady Anna back into the drawing-room. Lady Chesterton?"

The lady nodded and followed after Lady Hayward. Elias could hear them both murmuring encouragements to Lady Anna and felt his heart sink low in his chest. Just what had he done with his foolishness?

"I think," Lord Stevenson said quietly, looking at him with fury still burning in his gaze, "that it would be best if you returned home, Lord Comerfield."

Elias dropped his head. "Yes, of course," he muttered, all the more embarrassed that he was now, it appeared, being thrown from the dinner party due to his foolish behavior. "I quite understand."

"I am sorry," Lord Stevenson continued, without even a hint of an apologetic tone in his voice, "but I must consider Lady Anna. She is distressed enough without having to pretend all is well for the rest of the evening whilst you sit across from her."

"I quite understand," Elias replied, lifting his head and choosing to look his host full in the face. "Forgive me for making such difficulties at your dinner party, Lord Stevenson. It was not a deliberate act."

"So you keep saying," Lord Stevenson answered, his voice hard, "but that does not mean that your actions in themselves were not purposeful." His jaw worked hard for a moment and he looked away. "No doubt you believed her to be Lady Robertson."

Elias swallowed hard, heat creeping up his spine and into his neck. "Indeed."

"Then you should know that she has been making all manner of flirtations with Lord Heseltine, who is now sitting by her in the drawing-room," Lord Stevenson said, his dislike entirely unmasked. "Do not consider yourself to be her only thought, Lord Comerfield. It appears that you were nothing more than a passing activity for her to enjoy."

Lord Stevenson said nothing further, giving a short, sharp bow before turning on his heel and making his way back to the drawing-room. Elias watched him depart as all manner of emotion crashed down upon his head, leaving him feeling broken and ashamed. Turning on his heel, he made his way to the front of the house, snapping his fingers at one of the footmen and demanding his carriage be brought as though he were in some haste to leave rather than the truth of being thrown from the dinner party in disgrace.

Climbing inside, Elias directed his driver to take him home. He had no desire to got to Whites or to any other establishment, not when he had such a burden of guilt placed around his neck. The look on Lady Anna's face when she had turned to face him, when he had realized that she was *not*, in fact, Lady Robertson, was etched in his memory, grating at him and making him wish he had never set eyes on Lady Robertson that evening. Had he not seen her, then mayhap he would have returned to the drawing-room without hesitation, without even *considering* that he ought to put his arms around her and see what followed.

Groaning, Elias closed his eyes. He would have to wait until tomorrow, at least, before he knew what the *ton* would be saying of the incident, if anything. He prayed that the remaining guests at Lord Stevenson's dinner party would not be inclined to ask any questions, would not make the connection between his absence and Lady Anna's obvious upset. He prayed that Lady Chesterton would be willing to remain silent about the matter, despite her clear fury over his actions, and that Lord Stevenson himself would not be at all inclined to mention it either but would give another explanation for Elias' absence.

It will all be well, he told himself, trying to convince himself of such a statement. *You will return to society tomorrow and it will be as though nothing ever occurred. Perhaps you will need to write to Lady Anna and beg her forgiveness once more but there will be nothing more required of you.* Taking in a deep breath, Elias let it rattle out of him slowly, trying to find the confidence and assurance he needed to believe such statements. The truth was, he was dreadfully afraid that it would all turn out to be something of a disaster and that he would find himself caught in the middle of it all, with nowhere else to turn.

CHAPTER FOUR

Anna lifted terrified eyes towards her father as he came into the drawing-room, her teacup lying cold and forgotten in front of her. Behind him came Lady Hayward, whose reassuring smile did nothing to encourage Anna in any way, given the hard look on the duke's expression.

"My dear," the duke began, calming Anna's fears just a little. "Lady Hayward has told me of what happened last evening. I must say, I am more than a little upset!"

Anna swallowed hard, leaning forward in her chair as her fingers folded and unfolded the fabric of her skirts. "Father, I did not mean to—"

"He has no anger towards you, Lady Anna," Lady Hayward interrupted quickly, as the duke turned to look first at Lady Hayward and then back at Anna, his eyes widening just a fraction. "There is no need to worry."

"Indeed, there is not!" the duke reassured her as Anna let out a long breath of relief. "I have no anger towards your actions, my dear girl. You went to the retiring room and, upon your return, appear to have been held back by a gentleman who ought to have known better!"

Tension began to ripple through Anna's frame, pushing away from her as she looked into her father's face and saw his expression gentle. It was clear, then, that he had no anger towards *her*, which was more of a relief than she could express. Once more, she felt tears come into her eyes but, given that she had spent most of the night upset, afraid of what her father would say, Anna pushed them back with an effort as her father smiled gently.

"No, you have nothing to fear, Anna," he said with a good deal more warmth in his voice. "I am sorry if you believed me to be upset and angry with your behavior, for I can assure you that it is not so. It is with Lord Comerfield that I hold my grudge!" His jaw set firm, his eyes growing a little cold now. "Tell me, do you think that he intends to wed you?"

Anna let out a startled gasp, looking to Lady Hayward, who merely smiled and lifted one shoulder in a half-shrug.

"I—I should not think so, Father," she said quickly, thinking to herself that such an idea was horrific and praying that it would not be forced upon her. "After all, the intention was not to speak of what occurred, and Lady Chesterton, at least, managed not to say a word to any of the other guests." Whilst that in itself was true, Anna knew that the keen looks that had been sent her way by Lady Chesterton, as well as the fact that Lord Comerfield had been notable by his absence, had made some of the other guests very aware of the fact that something untoward had occurred, although, of course, they had all been much too polite to ask.

"That is true," Lady Hayward answered as the duke turned to glance at her before turning his now worried expression back towards Anna. "I believe we must wait to see what the *beau monde* says about this matter." She sighed and sat down in a chair next to Anna. "Whilst Lady Chesterton was very good at saying very little last evening, I am not convinced that her fortitude will continue."

Anna's eyes flared as panic struck her heart. "What do you mean, Lady Hayward?"

"I mean," Lady Hayward replied calmly, "that there will be those who seek to speak to her about what she saw last evening. She may wish to say very little, and indeed, her intentions might well be to remain entirely silent about such things, but my fear is that she will not be able to remain so for long. She will say that her upset and her anger towards Lord Comerfield were burning within her with such force that she was unable to keep quiet any longer and, no doubt, will speak quite openly about what she witnessed."

"And the *ton* will then whisper all manner of things about you and Lord Comerfield," the duke muttered, passing one hand over his eyes. "I am sorry, Anna. It appears as though you might well have to wed Lord Comerfield if it comes to it."

The panic that had spread through Anna's heart at Lady Hayward's words now redoubled itself. She did not like Lord Comerfield and had very little time for his company. What he had done last evening only added to her dislike of him, and now to be told that she might have to consider marriage to him was utterly horrifying!

"We will have to wait and see what the *ton* does, however," the duke continued, perhaps seeing the fear in her eyes. "I know this hardly seems particularly fair when you did nothing wrong, Anna, but it is the best way, unfortunately. Besides," he continued with a small shrug, "it is not as though he is a lowly baron or some such thing. He is a Marquess, and that, certainly, is something to be glad of."

Anna shook her head mutely, unable to find even a single word to speak in response. She could not be glad of his title, not when his character was of such low opinion! She would always resent him for his actions, would remain upset with him for forcing her into such a position whilst he, she was sure, would never be glad that a marriage had been forced upon him.

"Let us hope that Lady Chesterton remains quite silent," Lady Hayward said softly, bringing a small spark of hope to Anna's heart as she looked at her chaperone, desperate to find some sort of solace. "It may all be just as we hope, Lady Anna, and only a few guests from last evening will speak of what they saw without making any connection to Lord Comerfield."

Nodding, Anna took in a shuddering breath and closed her eyes, letting it out slowly in an attempt to calm herself. "How long must I wait, Lady Hayward?"

The lady considered for a moment, looking at the duke as she thought. "I think it would be best to go into town this afternoon," she said quietly, "and then to whatever occasion we are engaged in this evening—the evening assembly, is it not?"

"It is," Anna answered, finding no joy in the prospect. "You believe I should just go about my business as usual? Pretend that all is well?"

"All *is* well," the duke interrupted before Lady Hayward could respond. "You have done nothing wrong, Anna. It may be as Lady Hayward has suggested and nothing shall be said save for a few whispers."

"And if it is not?" Anna asked, turning to look at her father. "Then what shall I do?"

His expression was one of both sympathy and anger, for his eyes were bright with obvious fury towards Lord Comerfield, whilst soft at the edges as he looked back at her. A small smile lifted the corners of his mouth as he spread his hands, trying, it seemed, to be both honest and encouraging in equal measure.

"We will make such a decision when we must," he told her quietly. "Go with Lady Hayward into town and see what occurs. But Anna, you must not appear to be at all upset, not in any way. The *beau monde* must see you as you always are—confident, determined, and carefree. Do you understand me?"

Anna closed her eyes and nodded, not at all sure she could behave in such a way and yet realizing she must. She did not want the *ton* to add to their whispers simply by looking at her and realizing just how upset she was. She had to hide her true expression, had to pretend all was just as usual. No mention would be made of Lord Comerfield, and, should they meet any particular acquaintances, she would have to remain as silent as she could about the gentleman.

"Very well, Father," she answered a trifle hoarsely. "I will do as you ask."

The duke smiled, came towards her, and dropped a kiss to her forehead—such a rare expression of affection that Anna felt tears spring into her eyes as he stepped back from her. Her heart ached furiously but she said nothing to him, managing a watery smile as he looked down at her with clear sympathy in his eyes.

"I should return to my study and leave you to the care of Lady Hayward," he said, a trifle gruffly as though that was more than enough emotion for him at present. "Have no fear, my dear girl. We will make things come to rights in the end."

"I thank you, Father," Anna replied, watching her father as he turned and made his way to the door, pausing only to murmur one or two things into Lady Hayward's ear. Lady Hayward listened attentively and then nodded, looking up at the duke for a long moment before, finally, he took his leave. Wondering what had been said, Anna contained herself until the duke closed the door tightly behind him before bursting into a great flood of tears.

"Oh, my dear!" Lady Hayward exclaimed, coming towards her and putting her hand on Anna's arm, pulling out a handkerchief with her other hand and placing it in Anna's lap. "You have been through a very great deal. I am so very sorry."

Anna tried to dry her tears but found she could not, and thus, she permitted herself to cry openly for some minutes until, finally, they began to abate. The handkerchief lay as a sodden mess on her lap, but Lady Hayward picked it up in a very practical manner and, folding it up, set it on the table next to Anna's cold teacup.

"Well, we cannot go into town yet!" she remarked as Anna tried to smile. "You must prepare yourself, my dear. It will be difficult, yes, but it may come to naught."

Anna swallowed the ache in her throat and nodded, looking down at her lap. "I was so very afraid that my father would consider me to bear some of the responsibility in this matter," she said, her voice rasping a little. "That he would find that my behavior or some such thing was incorrect."

"Not at all," Lady Hayward answered firmly. "When I spoke to him, his only concern was for you. He did not even suggest that you had done anything wrong, my dear girl. You have done nothing worthy of punishment, so do not even permit your own heart to take on a guilt it does not deserve."

For whatever reason, these words seemed to bring Anna a kind of comfort and she nodded, taking in another long breath and finding herself a little more composed.

"No doubt, Lord Comerfield will have to speak to your father, one way or the other," Lady Hayward continued, rising to her feet and making her way back to her chair, pausing only to ring the bell. "He will have to give his explanation and his apology to your father directly."

Anna shuddered. "I should not like to be in his company again."

"But you cannot make it apparent that you are avoiding him," Lady Hayward warned. "Recall that we must make the *ton* believe, as best we can, that there is nothing of note between yourself and Lord Comerfield, even if the opposite is true." With a small sigh, she shook her head. "But do also prepare yourself for the possibility that the *ton* might whisper of you and that rumors might abound—to the point that the only course of action will be to pursue marriage."

A tight hand grasped Anna's heart, but she did not look away from Lady Hayward, wanting to face the truth without too much fear, even if her stomach lurched in a most uncomfortable fashion. "And Lord Comerfield will do such a thing?"

"I cannot see how he cannot, should it be required of him," Lady Hayward answered quietly. "But let us hope it will not be so." With a small smile, she gave herself a shake and then rose. "Now, you will have to take tea and cakes, I think, in order to settle your stomach and bring a little more color to your face. Thereafter, we will change and make our way into town, to perhaps sit at Gunter's or some such thing."

The thought of going into the *ton* was a frightening one, but Anna knew she could not hide away in her father's townhouse. "Very well," she answered, trying to hide her fear. "And if it is worse than we fear? If it is obvious that the *beau monde* now consider me in a much poorer light?"

Lady Hayward gave her a small, sympathetic smile. "Then we will consider what to do, should that situation arise," she said kindly. "But for now, rest and recover yourself, Lady Anna. Tea and cakes will arrive soon."

~

STEPPING out into the streets of London was more nerve-wracking than Anna had expected. Her sister had been murmuring words of encouragement whilst Lady Hayward had said nothing but merely watched Anna carefully as though afraid she might lose her composure completely in a single moment. However, having rested as Lady Hayward had suggested and having eaten a little something so as to steady her nerves, Anna felt more prepared for what she had to do.

The moment her foot hit the pavement, however, all courage left her. It felt as though everyone walking by her was looking at her as though she were the sole point of everyone's attention. It took all of her strength to remain where she was rather than climb back into the carriage to hide.

"There we are," Lady Hayward remarked, briskly. "Now, where shall we make for first? Gunter's? A book-shop? Or perhaps you should like to find something new to purchase?"

"Anything would suit me," Anna said before Lady Selina could answer. "I do not wish to linger out of doors for too long."

"Come now," Lady Hayward replied firmly. "Do not be too afraid, Lady Anna. You might very well find that those in the *ton* do not think poorly of you but rather think ill of Lord Comerfield!" Looking at Lady Selina, she smiled calmly. "What would your preference be, Lady Selina?"

"The bookshop would be quiet, certainly," Lady

Selina replied, clearly considering what Anna would need rather than her own preference—for which Anna was very grateful indeed. "Although I should like to search for a new pair of evening gloves at some point."

Lady Hayward nodded. "Then let us go there first," she said, directing them to a milliner's shop just behind Anna. "Yes, the bookshop will be quiet, but we do not want anyone to believe that you are hiding now, Lady Anna."

Anna swallowed hard, looking back at Lady Hayward. "No, indeed not," she answered miserably, knowing full well that to give such an impression would only make the *ton* believe that she was guilty of something, should they have heard of what had occurred last evening.

"Lift your chin a little and do not look at the ground," Lady Hayward instructed, studying Anna with a sharp eye. "If anyone greets you, then greet them in a calm manner and with a smile, if you can. Behave as though this is another day within society, and I shall be by your side should anything untoward occur."

Fear trapped itself in Anna's heart as she tried to do as Lady Hayward suggested. Turning herself towards the milliner's shop, she lifted her chin a notch, set her shoulders, and did her best to make her way towards it without showing any sign of nervousness. Lady Selina walked beside her with Lady Hayward just a step or two behind, and, much to her relief, she managed to make it into the shop without incident. No one stopped her. No one greeted her, and it was with relief that she began to peruse the items within, just as she might normally do.

"Is that Lady Anna?"

The first whisper came to Anna's ears within minutes. She froze, one hand settling on a blue ribbon, her eyes staring down at it intently without her ever really seeing it. Quite who had whispered such a thing, she did not know, but there was, clearly, an awareness that she was of importance to the *beau monde* at present.

"It is Lady Anna, yes."

Much to Anna's shock, the hard voice of Lady Hayward filled the milliner's shop. "Although quite why you are whispering about her, I cannot imagine!"

Slowly, Anna turned to look at Lady Hayward, who was speaking directly to two young ladies who had been standing only a few yards away from her, clearly the ones who had been whispering about her. Her face turned scarlet as she saw the two young ladies stare at her, their eyes wide as though she were a creature they had never seen before.

"Where is your chaperone?" Lady Hayward asked, finally dragging the two ladies' attentions back towards her. "I must ask them if they are aware as to why such whispering is taking place."

The first young lady dropped her head in evident embarrassment, whilst the second returned Lady Hayward's look with one of her own. "She is gone to call the carriage," she said, a little tartly. "And will return presently."

"Then I shall wait to speak to her," Lady Hayward replied, a hard glint coming into her eye. "For as I have said, there is no reason for you to be whispering about Lady Anna."

"That is not what is being said," replied the second, making Anna flush all the more with embarrassment. "It is said that Lady Anna was discovered last evening with a gentleman."

"And you take such rumors and simply accept them as such?" Lady Hayward asked, a hint of anger in her voice now. "Might I ask if either of you were present last evening, at the dinner party myself, Lady Selina, and Lady Anna attended?"

The two young ladies looked at each other, a frown burrowing across the second young lady's forehead. "I cannot imagine what you mean," she said in that same tone of voice that spoke of very little regard for Lady Hayward. "Of course we were not."

"Then might I suggest," Lady Hayward said firmly, "that you refrain from speculating and from listening to nothing more than idle gossip that, if permitted to spread as you seem very intent on doing, can ruin the reputation of a young lady who has done nothing wrong." She made to say more but was prevented from doing so by the opening of the shop door and, turning around, saw the startled face of an older lady whom, Anna considered, must be the chaperone of the young ladies.

Aware of the heat still in her cheeks and the embarrassment that held her in its tight grasp, Anna turned away as she heard Lady Hayward begin to speak to the young ladies' chaperone, although she had to confess she was a little relieved at the exclamation that came from the lady's mouth as she heard what her charges had been doing.

"My profound apologies!" came the voice of the

chaperone. "Miss Dolton—you will express an apology to both Lady Hayward and Lady Anna."

Anna winced but forced herself to turn back around, aware that she could not remain where she was, not when the lady in question was evidently to speak to her. She looked into the cool, calculating eyes of the young Miss Dolton and felt her heart sink.

She was lost.

"My sincere apologies," Miss Dolton murmured, clearly not at all heartfelt in what she said, given that her lip curled slightly and a look of distaste still etched itself into her expression. "I should not have spoken about you in such a manner."

"Indeed you should not," Anna found herself saying, suddenly determined to defend herself to this young lady, even though she knew it was not worth it given that Miss Dolton seemed quite determined to believe what she had heard. "As Lady Hayward states, I have done nothing wrong. Why then should the *beau monde* turn its back to me?" With another lift of her chin, she bobbed a quick curtsy to the as yet unintroduced chaperone and stalked away from the two young ladies, leaving their chaperone to remove them from the shop.

However, despite her outward appearance of strength, inside, Anna was crumbling. It was quite clear to her now, with that one particular encounter, that she would not be widely accepted by the *ton*. Someone had said something, and from that, a story had grown so that it now spread itself all across London society. Anna had no doubt that there would be news of her supposed poor behavior spreading through the *ton* at this very moment, although she prayed that not everyone would believe it.

"Are you quite all right, Anna?"

Lady Selina's anxious face came into view as she hurried towards Anna, clearly having overheard what had been said.

"I am...not," Anna said honestly, dropping her head and squeezing her eyes closed. "It seems that it is as I feared."

"Lady Chesterton must have been unable to remain silent," Lady Selina replied, putting out one hand to Anna's shoulder. "But that does not mean that everyone in the *ton* will believe it."

It was a small comfort. Even if some of the *beau monde* believed the rumors, then she would no longer be acknowledged by some of society. And she a duke's daughter!

"Lady Hayward is doing all she can to suppress it," Lady Selina continued, obviously attempting to be helpful and encouraging. "She has told you not to hide away, Anna. I think it is best to do as she suggests, no matter how difficult it may be."

Anna nodded but did not quite manage to hide her tears from her sister. Lady Selina murmured something sympathetic and then embraced Anna for a moment, before pulling out her handkerchief and handing it to her.

Anna managed to regain her composure with an effort, dabbing her tears away hurriedly. "It is all so very unfair," she said hoarsely. "I have done nothing wrong. I was returning from the retiring room, that is all! And yet now, I am the one who is being punished for Lord Comerfield's actions!"

"I know," Lady Selina replied gently. "And you are right, it is most unfair. But be glad that there are those within the *ton* who will believe you are speaking the truth, my dear sister. Father does not think you in the wrong. Lady Hayward knows that you are entirely innocent, as do Lord Stevenson and Lady Chesterton. There will be others who, knowing of Lord Comerfield's reputation as a flirtatious gentleman, will be inclined to consider *him* poorly, rather than yourself." She smiled. "You must take courage. And I, certainly, shall not neglect you either."

Swallowing hard, Anna nodded and tried to find the words to thank her sister, only for Lady Hayward to come to join them.

"Well!" she exclaimed, her eyes bright with anger and her lips pulled tight. "I should think that Miss Dolton—and by that, I mean the elder of the two sisters—will consider carefully the next time she decides to speak with such ridiculous abandon and listen to such foolish rumors," she finished, her hands planted on her hips.

"I thank you, Lady Hayward," Anna managed to say. "Although I am not certain that it will do much good."

"Nonsense," Lady Hayward replied firmly. "We will quash that ridiculous rumor if we must. *That* shall be our goal, Lady Anna. I will not have you belittled in the eyes of society when it is clear that you have done nothing wrong."

"That is just what I have said," Lady Selina added, her hand gently pressing Anna's. "There will be those in society who lean towards pressing the guilt to Lord Comerfield rather than to Anna."

Lady Hayward nodded, her hands slipping from her hips as she began to calm herself a little more. "Indeed," she said, speaking much more softly. "I will speak to your father again, Lady Anna, and encourage him to attend with us this evening, for I am certain he is included in the invitation. That will show the *ton* that the duke himself does not consider his daughter to be guilty of any such misdemeanors! And, for the moment, if you have the courage, we will step out back into London and continue on our way, just as planned." She spread her hands. "However, if you would prefer to return home, then I will be contented to accompany you there also."

Both Lady Selina and Lady Hayward looked at Anna with equal expressions of concern, waiting for her to make her decision. Anna did not know what to do, for everything in her wanted to return home, to hide away and to pray that, somehow, when she emerged, the rumors would be gone. But a small, quiet whisper reminded her that, should she do so, she would be giving credence to the gossip about her and that, in attempting to do as Lady Hayward had suggested, she would be showing the *beau monde* that she was not going to retreat, was not about to remove herself from them because she knew, full well, that she had done nothing wrong.

The memory of Lord Comerfield's hands on her waist, the warmth of his breath as it had brushed across her cheek, and the way his body had pressed to hers came back to her with full force, and she closed her eyes tightly, letting out a shuddering breath. There was no excitement in that memory, no joy nor happiness but only dread, regret, and shame. It did not matter that he had thought her to be another, did not matter that he believed her to be willing to accept his advances. What he had done, he had done, and now, it seemed she was to bear the consequences.

Another chill ran through her as she realized that she might very well have to consider an offer of marriage from Lord Comerfield, should things become very bad indeed. Was that something she dared risk? Or would she attempt to do as Lady Hayward had asked, in the hope that the rumors would fade almost as soon as they had sprung up and return her to a life of contentment and freedom?

"Very well, Lady Hayward," she said softly. "I will continue on as we had planned, in the hope that my courage, such as it is, does not fail me."

Lady Hayward beamed at this and reached across to press Anna's arm. "A very brave decision, my dear," she said kindly, although the gleam in her eye told Anna that Lady Hayward was all the more ready to demand an apology from anyone who might say something to Anna about her supposed behavior. "And one that, I hope, will prove itself to have been the right one, in the end."

"There is nothing else I can do," Anna replied a little heavily. "If I return home, I fear I shall never leave there again and what will become of me then?" She gave a small, wane smile to her sister, who nodded her agreement. "Then it is to the bookshop next, I believe, and then Gunter's?"

"Pray tell us immediately if you wish to return

home," Lady Hayward said as she began to make her way to the door. "There will be no shame in it, Lady Anna."

"No," Anna replied, managing to find her resolve, albeit a weak one. "No, I shall not rush home and away from the whispers. I must face them. I must show that I am not the one to be considered guilty."

Lady Hayward smiled and nodded, the door open for Anna to walk through. "Very good, Lady Anna," she answered softly. "Then let us hope your courage will be rewarded, just as it ought."

CHAPTER FIVE

Walking into the rooms that had been hired for Lord Paton's evening assembly, Elias felt an almost palpable chill run over him as he saw the many faces turning towards him. There then came the immediate whispers, the gloved hands lifted and pressed to the mouths of those who, he knew, were speaking only of him.

Closing his eyes for a moment, Elias picked up a glass of champagne and made his way across the room, desperate to find a familiar face.

"There he is!"

Elias turned his head, spotting an old acquaintance who was gesturing for Elias to join him. Relieved, Elias drew nearer, glad that he would not have to face the dark stares of many of the ladies of the *ton*.

"We were just speaking of you, Lord Comerfield!" Lord Jefferies cried, slapping Elias on the back. "It is all over London, and we had to hear it for ourselves!"

Elias blinked rapidly, looking at Lord Jefferies with a small frown. "What can you mean?"

"About your attempts to steal affections from a particular young lady," Lord Jefferies said with a chuckle as the other gentlemen laughed and muttered amongst themselves. "That did not go particularly well, I fear, although we commend you for attempting to do so! The daughter of a duke, indeed!" He laughed again as though it was nothing more than a joke rather than the serious matter that Elias knew it to be.

"She spurned you, however?" asked another gentleman as Elias felt himself grow a little angry, his spine straightening as he rose to his full height. "How unfortunate!"

"I did not realize it was Lady Anna," Elias replied tightly. "It was a misunderstanding and one that I am truly sorry for."

Much to his frustration, however, the gentlemen guffawed at this remark, shaking their heads as though he was being more than a little foolish.

"You cannot try to find any sort of excuse that will pardon you, Lord Comerfield!" cried another as Elias' frown deepened all the more. "It was a failure on your part, certainly, but one that I shall commend you for nonetheless! Attempting to steal her affections so that you might boast of it thereafter is quite extraordinary."

Elias' jaw worked furiously. Whoever it was that had spoken of his foolishness—no doubt, Lady Chesterton, given her manner—had managed to, inadvertently, given rise to many rumors about both himself and Lady Anna. The shame that had burned through his soul last evening returned with force, striking through him hard. It was not Lady Anna's fault in any way, and yet he knew she would be bearing the consequences of it.

"It was, as I have said, an accident," he said again, his dark tone of voice seeming to make the gentlemen realize that he was speaking truthfully. "I have never sought out the affections of any debutantes or the like. In the gloom —and given that I was a little overcome with liquor—I mistook her for another." He did not want to say who, given that such a statement would only upset matters further. "Lady Anna should bear no shame, given that the mistake was entirely mine."

No one replied to him for a moment or two, only for Lord Jefferies to break the awkward tension by shrugging and chuckling loudly. "Well, it is much too late for apologies or excuses," he said nonchalantly. "There will be those within the *beau monde* who will refuse to be in company with Lady Anna, and that is just the way of things."

Elias shook his head. "The rumors must be quashed."

Another gentleman snorted in derision. "That is hardly likely," he said with a roll of his eyes. "You know what the rumor mill is like, Comerfield! And besides, what does it matter?"

The anger that had begun to subdue itself once more rose within Elias' chest. "What do you mean?"

The gentleman shrugged. "She is the daughter of a duke. The gossip might cling to her, yes, but her father will be able to find a match for her somewhere."

Elias closed his eyes and, before he said something that would only cause more anger, turned away from them all and began to make his way, heedlessly, through the crowd of guests. He did not want Lady Anna to simply be given a match to cover over the consequences of what had been *his* foolishness. He had seen such matches being made before—matches where the lady in question had been wed to a gentleman who did not care anything for her save for the dowry she would bring. A gentleman who might be many years older, who might have already been wed and then become a widower later in life. How could he step aside and allow such rumors to inflict injuries upon Lady Anna when he was the one responsible?

Groaning, he made to sit down heavily in a chair by the side of the room, where the wallflowers and companions gathered, only to spot the very lady in question moving towards him with her father by her side. Elias' stomach dropped. He had not behaved wisely thus far, he realized, for no doubt, he should have gone directly to the duke and apologized for his foolishness. Instead, he had spent the day at his townhouse, reveling in his shame and disgrace. He had hoped that there would be no rumors swirling about the *ton* by the evening, had prayed desperately that Lady Chesterton and Lord Stevenson had kept their word to remain tightly lipped about what had occurred, but his hopes had been dashed.

Taking in a deep breath and hoping that his conversation with the duke would not be noticed by too many of the other guests, Elias made his way slowly towards him, his heart hammering furiously as he did so. It seemed that the duke noticed him before his daughter, for he threw him a glance and then continued on his way, before looking back towards Elias for the second time. It was then that Lady Anna caught his gaze, and, as she did so, she stumbled and her father was forced to catch her arm.

This did not bode well.

"Your Grace," Elias began, bowing low and, as he rose, keeping his eyes to the man's shoulder. "Lady Anna. Might I first begin by expressing my deep sorrow and my sincere regret for what occurred at the dinner party last evening. I must also apologize for not seeing an audience with you this afternoon, Your Grace, for I am well aware of my own shortcomings and the fact that I did not even consider coming to speak to you personally was very wrong of me and entirely inconsiderate towards you, Lady Anna."

The duke harrumphed loudly, interrupting Elias' speech. "Mayhap now is not the time to be speaking of such things, Lord Comerfield," he said, his voice calm but a hard gleam of steel in his eyes. "Might you call tomorrow?"

Elias swallowed his words and nodded.

"There is much to be discussed," the duke continued gruffly. "I am aware of what occurred and the fact that there was a misunderstanding. But that being said, Lord Comerfield, it does not excuse your behavior."

"Of course it does not," Elias agreed, nodding. "I would be glad to discuss things further with you, Your Grace, come the morrow." Turning to Lady Anna, he inclined his head, feeling the shame burning up within him. "And again, Lady Anna, I am truly sorry for all of this."

She said nothing but dropped her gaze, looking away

from him as her cheeks slowly colored. Elias took this as his cue to leave and stepped away from them both, making his way back to the chairs by the side of the room and, finding a vacant one, sitting down heavily. It felt as though everyone in the room was waiting for him to emerge, waiting for him to reveal himself so that they might all whisper about him once more. The gentlemen of the *ton*, on the whole, would not consider his actions a particularly grievous offense, but would either laugh about it, as Lord Jefferies had done, or shrug with a lack of interest. It was the ladies of the *ton* that would be spreading the gossip, speaking of it—and of him—to as many others as they could. And within that gossip would be Lady Anna, in their eyes as much to blame for it as he.

"So, you are present, but you are in hiding."

Elias grimaced. "I am not hiding," he lied as Lord Rowley shook his head in clear disbelief. "I am simply sitting here for a short time in order to gather my thoughts."

"Is that so?" Lord Rowley murmured, sitting down next to him. "Might I say, your thoughts appear to be most melancholy."

"Perhaps they are," Elias muttered, looking away from his friend. "You have heard the rumors, then?"

Lord Rowley nodded. "Of course."

"They are not true!" Elias exclaimed, his head snapping sharply to his left as he glared at Lord Rowley as though he had already said that he believed every word of each bit of gossip he had heard. "Lady Anna was not to blame."

Lord Rowley waited for a moment before nodding. "I

did not think she was," he replied quietly. "I am surprised at your vehemence, however."

Elias closed his eyes. "It is because of what I know will now come to her because of my foolishness," he said heavily as the weight of his guilt settled upon him once more. "I thought her Lady Robertson."

"I do not think it matters *who* you thought her to be," Lord Rowley replied grimly. "The fact is, you have made a serious misstep and there must now be considerations for the lady herself."

Frowning, Elias felt a tight ball of anxiety swirl about his heart. "What can you mean? I have already spoken to a good many gentlemen and made it quite clear that she was not to blame in any way."

"That will do no good!" Lord Rowley snapped dismissively, clearly irritated by Elias' lack of consideration. "If you are to make amends, if you are to secure her reputation and return her to society's good graces, then you know there is only one choice."

Elias sucked in a breath. "You are not considering that I should ask her to marry me?" he said, a little surprised when Lord Rowley nodded. "Come now, it is not as serious as all that! It was a mistake, that is all." Panic began to clasp at his heart and he shook his head fervently as though doing so would convince Lord Rowley that he was in the wrong. "You know that I could not wed her."

"Why ever not?" Lord Rowley asked, his voice rising with his temper. "That is what you *ought* to propose, given that you have brought her so low!"

"Because it would not bring about any happiness nor

contentment for either of us!" Elias replied sharply. "I have already planned to meet with her father tomorrow, and, at that point, we shall come up with a plan as to what we are to do next."

Shaking his head, Lord Rowley pushed himself up from his chair, his lips in a thin line as his eyes narrowed. "Someday soon, mayhap even tomorrow, you will discover that what I have stated is precisely what the duke expects," he said, darkly, his gaze never quite settling on him. "Prepare yourself, Lord Comerfield, for the duke *will* ask you to consider matrimony."

Elias scoffed at this. "I hardly think he will want his daughter to wed a scoundrel such as me," he replied as Lord Rowley shook his head and turned away from him. "Not when I was the one who placed her in such difficulties." He did not tell Lord Rowley that the very thought of matrimony terrified him and that, as such, he had no eagerness to join himself with any young lady, even if it was Lady Anna.

"You are a coward *and* a fool," Lord Rowley murmured, his head turning back towards Elias, no happiness nor understanding in his expression. "I believe that you will find the duke very encouraged towards matrimony, even though you are responsible for his daughter's current difficulties." He lifted one shoulder. "It is the only way to restore her, save to marry her off to someone else—but who would want to align themselves with a young lady who has *apparently* behaved as she?" His voice held a note of warning as he finished speaking, his eyes narrowing and his hand tightening on the glass he held. "You are responsible, Comerfield. Do your duty."

Those words echoed around Elias' head for the rest of the night. He did not linger for long at the evening assembly, finding himself so deeply confused and confounded that he was forced to depart in the hope of finding a little solace in the quietness of his house. However, even in the night, Elias was unable to find the peace he so desired. Minute after minute, he could see nothing but Lady Anna's white face and hear nothing but Lord Rowley's words.

Do your duty.

"You say that you mistook my daughter for another."

Elias lowered his eyes. "That is so, Your Grace," he replied without any hesitation. "I will be truthful and state that there are those within society who are a little freer with their favors."

The duke's brows lowered heavily over his eyes. "Something I am well aware of, Lord Comerfield, as I am also quite certain that my daughter is not one of them!"

"No, indeed, she is not," Elias replied hastily. "She has similar coloring to that of the lady who had been making certain...suggestions towards me earlier that evening and, I confess, that within my slightly addled mind, I thought Lady Anna to be her."

The duke's frown grew darker. "Addled?" he repeated. "You mean, you were in your cups."

Heat seared Elias' face. "Yes," he admitted. "I was not

thinking clearly, otherwise I am quite certain I would never have thought of doing such a thing."

Waving a hand, the Duke rose from his chair, eyeing Elias carefully. "Whether or not you would have normally behaved in such a manner does not interest me, Lord Comerfield," he replied heavily. "It is what we are to do now that is of concern. For it seems that, despite the efforts of Lady Hayward, the rumor is that you were embracing my daughter and she was willingly in your arms. That, of course, is preposterous, and I am glad, certainly that there are some who do *not* believe it, but that does not mean that my daughter has not been adversely affected by your actions."

"I am very aware of that," Elias stated, not shirking from his responsibility. "I have given the matter some consideration and I have come up with what I hope is the very best solution for Lady Anna."

The duke lifted one eyebrow, his gaze piercing as he fixed it upon Elias. "And what might that be?"

Elias took in a deep breath. If the Duke did not give the matter any consideration whatsoever, then he would have no other choice but to propose marriage, and that was the very last thing he wanted to do.

"I know that the usual expectation is for myself to propose marriage to Lady Anna," he said, his stomach tightening at the prospect. "However, I am not convinced that such an agreement would be for the best, particularly since I am fully aware that Lady Anna is less than pleased with me."

"Understandably," the Duke muttered, to which Elias could only nod.

"Therefore," he said, speaking a little more hurriedly, "I propose that in place of marriage, I find a way to assist Lady Anna back into society. I will have to discover a way to make certain that her reputation is fully restored, although I confess that I have not yet come to a full awareness of what I should do in order to do such a thing."

The Duke's frown was not particularly encouraging. "What you are trying to say, Lord Comerfield, is that you do not wish to wed my daughter and thus are attempting to find other ways to bring about a solution that will restore Lady Anna to society, even though such a thing will prove very difficult indeed."

Elias hesitated, unable to give an immediate response. He could tell that the duke was not at all impressed with his attempts to remove the thought of marriage from both his and the duke's mind.

"I have many friends within society who are of good standing," he said, choosing to ignore the Duke's question and instead continue to explain what he intended. "Lord Stevenson and Lady Chesterton, who were present during that unfortunate evening, are both inclined towards your daughter rather than to me. In short, Your Grace, there are those who will assist Lady Anna back into society, who will stand by her side without hesitation and prove to the *ton* that they do not believe the rumors."

"And their company, you hope, will be enough to push my daughter back into the fold," the Duke murmured, not looking at all convinced.

"In addition," Elias said hastily, "I know many excellent gentlemen who, I am sure, would be glad to be acquainted with your daughter." He saw the duke frown but pressed ahead regardless. "They will need an explanation from me, certainly, and I will not pretend that some won't need a little more convincing than others, but I am sure that I can have them in the company of Lady Anna very soon indeed."

The Duke let out a long breath and pinched the bridge of his nose, his eyes closed tightly for a moment. Elias said nothing at all, his stomach knotting itself with tension. Should the Duke refuse what was, he had to admit, a weak plan, then there would be no choice but for him to propose marriage to Lady Anna. That thought sent another flurry of fear down his spine as he waited for the duke to make his judgment, hating the very thought of marrying a lady he barely knew in order to salvage what was left of her reputation.

"I will be honest with you, Lord Comerfield, as you have been with me." The duke's voice was low and grave, his eyes a little hooded as he looked back at Elias. "There is nothing in this world I wish for more than the happiness of my daughters. It may appear as though I am very far from them, as though I care very little about their wellbeing given the situation with Lady Hayward, but the truth is that I have come to an agreement with her because I want the very best for my daughters. You, it seems, have taken away some of Lady Anna's happiness, as well as frustrating her chances at a successful match."

It has been for naught, Elias thought to himself, a cold hand grasping his heart. *I will have to wed the lady.*

"You are a marquess, and thus, your title is more than sufficient for one of my daughters," the duke continued as

Elias' spirits continued to sink low. "However, it is quite clear to me that your character is severely lacking in worth. In addition, my daughter does not have any desire to be forced into matrimony with you."

The sting of the duke's words were gentled only by the edge of relief that began to make its way into Elias' heart. His eyes lifted to the duke's as the man continued to speak, beginning, finally, to believe that he might be allowed to keep a hold of his freedom.

"Nonetheless, it is important that Lady Anna is not spurned by society entirely. Therefore, whilst I have listened to your intentions, I confess myself not entirely convinced that you will be able to improve things for my daughter." The duke took in a long breath, his lips pressing hard together for a moment so that they appeared almost entirely white. His eyes were narrowed as he studied Elias carefully, clearly making a decision that would affect Elias' future entirely.

"Therefore," the duke said, slowly, as Elias' heart began to pound furiously. "You will do what you can to ensure my daughter is returned to society and into their good graces, since she herself has done nothing worthy of their displeasure. But, if after a fortnight, you have not managed to make any progress whatsoever, then you shall offer marriage to my daughter."

For a moment, Elias could not breathe. The tension that had been coiling slowly around him now began to release the tight hold it had on his chest, and he found himself gasping for breath, lowering his head just a little.

"A fortnight might not be enough time," he found himself saying, even though he knew that every part of him ought to be thanking the duke for his willingness to permit such a thing. "Might I ask for a little more time?"

The duke's frown was a little angry. "Three weeks," he said, his voice grating hard now. "But no more."

Elias let out a long breath, closing his eyes for a moment as he took in what the duke had said. "I thank you, Your Grace," he said, fully aware that there was now a great deal of responsibility on his shoulders—but responsibility that he fully deserved. The duke was quite right to state that this was entirely his doing and, thus, it was also his responsibility to make certain that all he could do was done for Lady Anna. The fact that he would not have to wed her brought such relief that he could not speak for some moments, rising to his feet and lifting his head slowly so that he might converse honestly to the duke.

"Three weeks," he said, after another few moments. "Might I have your permission to also speak to Lady Anna to apologize, again, for what I have done and to assure her that I shall do all I can to make certain of her success?"

The duke nodded, his frown still remaining in place as he studied Elias, perhaps worrying that he had already made the wrong decision.

"She is waiting for my response to your visit," he said, a little coldly. "You may speak to her for a few minutes, Lord Comerfield." He let out a sigh as though he were deeply sorrowful over what had occurred, reminding Elias that he was entirely to blame for this situation. "You will find her in the parlor."

"I thank you," Elias murmured, bowing low. "You have been most understanding, Your Grace."

"And it has not been for your sake, Lord Comerfield," the duke replied. "I can tell you are reluctant to wed, Lord Comerfield, and it is for that reason, and that reason alone, that I have accepted your offer to attempt something different. I should not like my daughter wed to a gentleman who cares nothing for her, and it is for *her* sake that I have agreed to this." His jaw worked for a moment. "Do not fail, Lord Comerfield."

Elias swallowed hard, realizing that he was being held back from seeing the full extent of the duke's anger and upset. There was something of a threat in the duke's words, and Elias could not help but feel a growing anxiety settle over him. But, keeping his chin lifted and what he hoped was an assured expression on his face, he nodded and bowed low. "I thank you, Your Grace," he said again. "Do excuse me."

Walking out of the study and allowing the door to close behind him, Elias took a moment to draw in breath, feeling his heart begin to pound with yet another sense of growing tension. He had to make his way to the parlor now, to speak with the very lady who wanted nothing more to do with him. The lady he had wronged so very greatly. Shaking his head, he rubbed one hand across his eyes and then lifted it, looking along the hallway and steeling himself inwardly. Quite how Lady Anna would react, he did not know, but he had very little doubt that she would not be overly glad to see him. With a heavy sigh, he made his way along the hallway and to the parlor, praying that, at the very least, she would be relieved to hear that he would not have to wed her. Quite what she would say to knowing that he would be a little more in her company, guiding her as best he could to those in society who would be glad of her presence, he did not know, but it was the only way he could think of to make certain they avoided matrimony.

Steeling himself, Elias came to the door of the parlor, which was a little ajar. He heard the murmur of conversation and, after a moment, pushed the door open and stepped inside, ready to greet Lady Anna and whoever was with her. The time for him to speak was now at hand.

CHAPTER SIX

"I do not like this idea, Lady Hayward."

"I am not in the least bit surprised," Lady Hayward replied kindly, "but if the alternative is matrimony, then you must consider what is best."

Anna let out a long breath and nodded, looking out of the carriage window and praying silently that this evening would go as well as Lord Comerfield had promised. There was, however, a great deal of doubt within her heart that she would find herself welcomed, given how society had treated her at the ball only two nights ago, she did not think that things would immediately change.

"Lord Comerfield has promised this evening will have those within it who are much more inclined to believe you free of any guilt whatsoever and, thus, we are expected to have a very pleasant evening indeed," Lady Hayward reminded her as though she had forgotten. "Your father would not have agreed to this if he did not believe that there was a good chance of success."

Anna nodded but did not speak. She recalled the moment Lord Comerfield had come into the parlor, the way that he had dropped his head and greeted both herself and Lady Selina, who had been sitting quietly together engaged in gentle conversation about her situation at present. She had not expected to see him, had thought that, after his conversation with her father, he would depart the house and leave her to discuss matters further with her father. The shock that had rippled down her spine as he had come into the room had rendered her entirely mute for some minutes.

What he had told her had brought with it a measure of relief. Relief that she would not be forced to wed him, would not be expected to step forward and marry the gentleman who had caused her so much difficulty, and yet with that had come the fear that she would be left entirely to society's judgments. When he had explained to her what he intended to do, she had found herself staring at him in disbelief, for what could he do to aid her when he was the one who had behaved so poorly at the first? The words he had spoken had been rushed and, at times, a little jumbled, but slowly she had begun to understand that he intended to use the very best of his acquaintances to ensure that she was not entirely thrust from society. She had been assured that there were many within the *beau monde* who would quickly believe that he had been the one to behave inappropriately and that she needed only to give him time to make certain that she was surrounded by those who would not judge her, rather than being forced to wander through a ball and avoid almost every sharp look that came her way.

Three weeks.

Anna had to admit to herself that she had been less than convinced by Lord Comerfield's explanation of what he intended to do. In fact, the more he spoke, the less certain she became, but, as Lady Selina had reminded her thereafter, if this was the only opportunity available to her aside from stepping into a hasty engagement, then was it not worth considering? When he had told her that her father had agreed to only three weeks of this particular arrangement before a marriage would have to take place, she had felt a trembling take a hold of her frame for some moments. Three weeks did not seem to be a prolonged length of time, and yet, perhaps seeing the doubt on her face, Lord Comerfield had assured her that it was entirely possible and that he had every hope of success.

Thus, she now found herself in the carriage with Lady Selina and Lady Hayward, making their way to Lord and Lady Chesterton's evening soiree. They had previously received an invitation, of course, and whilst Lord Comerfield had also been issued one, Anna was not entirely sure that he would still be as welcome as before. Yet, he had promised her that, during this evening, he would do all he could to introduce her to some of his acquaintances in the hope that they would accept her and speak to her warmly, just as before this dreadful matter had taken hold.

She could not help but feel nervous.

"Recall that Lady Chesterton does not believe for one moment that you behaved in any wrong way," Lady

Hayward said kindly, as though she could see into the very depths of Anna's heart and mind and knew of her nervousness, her anxiety, and her fear. "If you have been invited, then it speaks plainly of Lord and Lady Chesterton's opinion of you, even if we are quite certain that it was Lady Chesterton who spoke of such a thing in the first place!"

Anna nodded but said nothing, her fingers twisting together as she held them tightly in her lap. As the minutes ticked by, she felt her nervousness grow all the more steadily, her heart pounding with such a fury that she was sure that her sister and Lady Hayward could hear it. But the carriage rumbled on slowly until, finally, they reached Lord and Lady Chesterton's townhouse. Anna wanted to cling to her seat, to tell the driver to turn around and return her home at once but knew she could not. Summoning as much of her courage as she could, she stepped down and looked up at the townhouse before her, trying to steel herself for what was to come, whatever it might be.

"Good evening, Lady Anna!"

Lady Chesterton's voice was just as loud as Anna recalled, and she did not miss the way that several heads swiveled towards them all as Lady Chesterton finished greeting both Lady Selina and Lady Hayward.

"I am so very glad that you chose to attend this evening," Lady Chesterton continued, speaking directly to Anna, who was forced to put a small smile on her face. "I know that you have had a great deal of difficulty these last few days, but I am here to assure you that you will find no such judgment from me."

"I thank you," Anna murmured, wishing that Lady Chesterton would not speak so loudly. "And also for your kind invitation. I am very glad to be here this evening." Forcing a smile to her lips to cover the lie, Anna waited until Lady Hayward was able to remove herself from Lady Chesterton's company and then walked a little further into the room, keeping her eyes fixed straight ahead.

The room was quite large, although Anna saw that there was an adjoining door open also, though where it led, she was not sure. Lady Hayward murmured a greeting to one or two people as they passed but continued to lead Anna and Selina towards a quieter part of the room, where, finally, they were able to catch their breath.

"Good evening, Lady Anna, Lady Selina."

A gruff voice caught her ears and Anna turned around to see none other than Lord Comerfield and, with him, Lord Rowley, whom she had already been introduced to.

"Good evening," she murmured as he greeted Lady Hayward also. "Good evening, Lord Rowley."

The gentleman's eyes were filled with sympathy as he looked back at her, inclining his head just a little. "Good evening, Lady Anna," he replied warmly. "And to you also, Lady Selina, Lady Hayward." Smiling at them both, he returned his gaze to Anna. "Lord Comerfield here has told me of his intention to help you return to society, Lady Anna. I do hope you have no concern with my assisting you with this also?"

Anna frowned. "I do not know what you mean."

"I am well aware of Lord Comerfield's lack of sense and decorum in what occurred," Lord Rowley answered without so much as glancing at Lord Comerfield as he spoke. "I have given him my opinion on the matter and have informed him of what I think he ought to do." This was accompanied by a tightening of his jaw and a sudden glare towards Lord Comerfield, who accepted such a look without protest. "However," Lord Rowley continued, looking back at Anna as the anger faded from his eyes, "he has informed me of the agreement between himself and your father and, thus, I have offered my assistance in this matter also."

A little surprised, Anna looked back at Lord Rowley with wide eyes. "That is very kind of you, Lord Rowley," she answered after a moment. "I am grateful for any friend that I might have here this evening."

Lord Rowley smiled, his face transforming into a bright, happy expression that made Anna smile back at him, in spite of the anxiety that still captured her heart.

"Then you can be assured of my friendship," he said honestly. "If that is quite all right, Lady Hayward?"

Lady Hayward laughed softly. "I should not reject you, Lord Rowley," she answered as Lady Selina watched carefully, her eyes fixed to Lord Rowley as though she were seeing him for the very first time. "Your kindness speaks very highly of your most excellent character and I am sure that Lady Anna will be very glad of your company any time you can spare it."

Lord Rowley inclined his head. "Wonderful," he said, giving a sideways glance to Lord Comerfield, who was neither smiling nor looking at all happy about the situation. "And whilst I believe that Lord Comerfield ought to have taken an entirely different action to settle this matter, I am glad to be of assistance with this particular endeavor."

Anna flushed, realizing that Lord Rowley expected Lord Comerfield to marry her without hesitation so that her reputation might be restored and, before she could prevent herself, found herself speaking with a good deal of honesty.

"I am grateful for the opportunity to avoid such a situation," she said as Lord Comerfield's eyes widened, looking at her with evident surprise. "But if it fails, then the course of action you speak of, Lord Rowley, is still expected to occur."

Lord Rowley chuckled, his eyes holding fast to hers. "Then I am glad you have been given such an opportunity, Lady Anna," he said as Lord Comerfield dropped his head, clearly a little embarrassed. "Now, should you wish it, I would be glad to sit with you during the musical portion of the evening, which will begin very soon, I believe."

Anna smiled back at him. "I would be most grateful," she answered as Lady Hayward nodded approvingly. "Thank you, Lord Rowley."

Inclining his head, he took his leave of her and stepped away, taking Lord Comerfield with him. Anna let out a long breath and felt some of her tension dissipate, realizing that, at least for this evening, she would have one friend present.

"Lord Rowley is an excellent gentleman, it seems," Lady Hayward murmured, one eyebrow lifting as she came to stand a little closer to Anna. "What do you think of him, Lady Anna?"

"Yes, indeed, he is very kind," Anna agreed only to see the gleam in Lady Hayward's eyes. "But I should not think that such kindness is meant as anything other than that, Lady Hayward. Let us not expect more of him than he is willing to give at present!" She had no inclination towards Lord Rowley, thinking him a very gracious and generous character but finding herself less than eager to pursue any sort of courtship or the sort with him. "What I am most concerned with at present is being a part of society again," she said as Lady Hayward nodded. "Let us focus on that rather than on thinking which gentleman, out of the few that still think well of me, might be a suitable match!"

Lady Hayward sighed but nodded, as Lady Selina smiled quietly, her eyes still on Lord Rowley.

"Besides which," Lady Selina murmured, keeping her voice very low indeed, "I believe that Lord Rowley is quite taken with another."

Anna frowned. "What can you mean?" she asked, only to see Lord Rowley bowing over the hand of a young lady, who was blushing furiously. When he smiled into her eyes, there was something in his expression that Anna had not seen when he had smiled at her. Evidently, Lady Selina, in her quiet observations, was quite correct.

"That is something of a pity," Lady Hayward said with a small sigh. "But we need not fix our intentions solely upon Lord Rowley. If, as Lord Comerfield has promised, you are to be introduced to others of his acquaintance who, evidently, believe him to be just as much a fool as he himself states, then there may be others who—"

"I cannot think of that at present, Lady Hayward," Anna interrupted, her anxiety getting the better of her as her voice became a little sharp. "It is enough for me simply to stand in this room with other guests and pray that even one or two of them will be willing to continue our acquaintance." Closing her eyes, she drew in a quick breath, her hands clenching into tight fists. "I fear that some may give me the cut direct."

When she opened her eyes, Lady Hayward was watching her with a calmness about her expression that immediately settled some of Anna's upset.

"I quite understand," Lady Hayward said gently. "Forgive me. I ought not to be pushing you towards any gentlemen, not when there is already enough difficulty for you at present."

Anna subsided. "I must hope that it will be as Lord Comerfield has said," she answered, feeling suddenly very tired indeed. "And if it is not, then I must face the realization that I am soon to be wed to him."

"Is that such a dreadful prospect?" Lady Selina asked as Anna jerked her head towards her, anger burning through her once more. "After all, he is a marquess, and, from what he is doing, there may well be something of a decent character to him, underneath the selfishness and arrogance that is so often displayed."

Biting back a harsh retort, it took all of Anna's will to remain silent as she fought against the urge to remind her sister that *she* had not been the one subjected to Lord Comerfield's advances. That she was not the one now facing such great difficulties and that she had no such concerns as Anna had.

"As much as I might wish to disagree, there is wisdom in considering Lord Comerfield," Lady Hayward agreed, speaking with infinite gentleness as though she could see the ball of fire that was currently lodged in Anna's heart. "It would bring an end to your difficulties at present, although I understand that such a thought is not at all pleasant."

"No," Anna replied tightly, no longer able to look at her sister or Lady Hayward. "It is not a pleasant thought at all, and I can assure you both that I have no intention of giving Lord Comerfield even a momentary consideration. Not until I am told that there is no other choice for me but to do so."

Lady Hayward nodded and said nothing more, leaving the three of them to stand in silence for a short time. Anna was torn between wanting to speak further, wanting to explain why she certainly could *not* consider Lord Comerfield, and having an urge to berate her sister for stating such a foolish thing in the first place.

Her thoughts were interrupted, however, by the arrival of three ladies who, coming towards them, stopped for a moment, murmuring to each other, before advancing closer.

Anna felt her heart sink, for there were matching supercilious smiles on each of the three faces. One, a lady she presumed was the mother of the younger two ladies, greeted Lady Hayward warmly, although Lady Hayward herself did not seem as delighted to receive the lady's company.

"Good evening, Lady Warwickshire," Lady Hayward murmured, glancing towards Lady Selina and then to Anna, a warning look in her eyes. "Might I present my charges? This is Lady Selina and Lady Anna, daughters to the Duke of Landon. Lady Anna, Lady Selina, might I introduce the Countess of Warwickshire."

Lady Warwickshire was a tall but plump woman, with small, narrowed eyes and a look of arrogance that passed from her to her daughters. Anna dropped into a curtsy at once, feeling her stomach tighten as she rose, seeing how the lady was watching her with sharp eyes.

"These are my two *wonderful* daughters," Lady Warwickshire replied, dragging the word out. "Lady Frederica and Lady Margaret."

"How very good to meet you," Lady Selina replied as Anna merely smiled, fairly certain that this was not a pleasant meeting. "Are you enjoying London at present?"

Lady Margaret glanced at her mother, who gave her a small nod, evidently giving her permission to answer.

"We are, very much," Lady Margaret replied, her eyes darting towards Anna even though she spoke to Lady Selina. "We have been very well instructed and have been doing very well indeed thus far in amongst society."

Lady Warwickshire seemed to glow with pleasure. "It is always a disappointment to hear when someone falls into disgrace," she said bluntly, "although I am relieved to know that it shall never be one of my two daughters! They have been, as Lady Margaret has said, *very* well prepared."

"As have we both," Anna found herself saying, aware of how hot her face was becoming but finding herself quite unable to remain silent. "One lesson that must be learned by being in London and in amongst the *ton*, however, is that rumors and such like cannot always be fully believed."

The color pulled itself from Lady Warwickshire's cheeks and she lifted her chin a notch, her lips thin and her eyes even more narrowed.

"Attempting to cover your poor behavior with poor excuses is not something that is at all proper, Lady Anna," she said briskly, turning her head away as though she could not even bear to look at her. "Most improper."

"I can assure you, Lady Warwickshire, that what Lady Anna states is quite true," Lady Hayward replied, a faint spot of color rising in each cheek. "And it is a wise lesson to learn, I think, for such rumor and gossip will, inevitably, bring harm to those who do not deserve it."

This made Lady Warwickshire snort with derision, and Anna's face flushed hot, making her close her eyes with embarrassment. It was clear that Lady Warwickshire's sole intention in joining them here was so that she might either ridicule Anna or show her daughters what could occur to a lady if one did not behave as properly as expected.

"I find your defense of Lady Anna utterly indefensible, Lady Hayward," Lady Warwickshire stated, lifting her chin a notch. "I brought my daughters here so that Lady Selina might be introduced to them, for my heart goes out to the poor young lady who is so tied to her sister and thus, will inevitably be tainted by her sister's short-comings." She shook her head and tutted loudly, as Anna opened her eyes to see her sister's face also red with either irritation or embarrassment but felt her own heart sinking low in her chest. Lady Warwickshire was quite correct in her statement. Lady Selina *would* be tainted by such rumors, even though it would be a great deal less than Anna herself.

"I do not need such assistance, however kindly meant," Lady Selina replied, her voice holding more determination than Anna had ever heard it. "I believe my sister's account of such matters and should you speak to Lord Comerfield—"

"Then he will tell you precisely the same thing."

Anna's gaze darted to her right, astonished to see Lord Comerfield standing there, clearly having just joined them. Had he been watching her? Had he heard Lady Warwickshire speak? Was he now truly coming to defend her in such an obvious manner?

"Lord Comerfield," Lady Warwickshire said, her lip curling as her two daughters took a small step back from him, their distaste apparent in both their expressions and their manner. "I hardly think that—"

"Lady Anna is entirely innocent of the spurious rumors that are currently making their way through the *ton*, Lady Warwickshire," he stated, interrupting her. "Therefore, I can assure you that the fault and the blame were entirely my own. I was, as much as it is embarrassing enough to admit, fully in my cups and did not know what I was doing." This, of course, was not precisely the truth, but, for the moment, Anna did not care about honesty. "She was making her way back from the retiring room and I was foolish in my actions indeed. If you are to spurn anyone, if you are to turn away from someone, then it ought, by rights, to be myself, Lady Warwickshire. Lady Anna is not to blame, and I shall not allow you to speak to her in such a manner when she has done nothing wrong."

It was a long speech, and when he finished, Anna could see that even those around them had gone quiet, their conversations halted so that they could overhear what Lord Comerfield would say in response to Lady Warwickshire. Instead of feeling any great pleasure at such a thing, instead of feeling herself glad that he had spoken, Anna felt awash with embarrassment. Dropping her head, she did not hear Lady Warwickshire's curt reply, such was the sound of blood roaring in her ears, her hands tightening together as she held them in front of her. Never before had she wanted to escape from such a conversation, feeling as though she were being imprisoned against her will.

"You take the blame entirely on yourself, Lord Comerfield, but I will not believe it," Lady Warwickshire replied after a few moments. "Your reputation speaks for itself, but I will not pretend that young ladies such as *this* are not easily persuaded by your charms. Attempting to restore her by stating that you are the only one responsible in such a situation may do something to satisfy your own guilt, but I shall not accept it."

With a toss of her head, she turned on her heel. "Come, girls."

Anna kept her head low as Lady Warwickshire and her daughters walked away from them all, feeling such mortification that she wanted to sink through the floor. She was in no doubt that many others were now speaking of what they had both witnessed and overheard, finding her heart so pained that tears sprang into her eyes.

"Are you quite all right, Lady Anna?" Lady Hayward was beside her in a moment, but Anna could not lift her head for fear of bursting into great sobs, which would only make things all the worse for her.

"Ridiculous woman!" came the voice of Lord Rowley, forcing Anna to blink back her tears. "Come now, Lady Anna, you must take heart. There are some ladies here whom Lord Comerfield knows would be glad to acquaint themselves with you."

Anna shook her head. "No, I thank you," she answered, her voice barely louder than a whisper. "I have no desire to be introduced to anyone else."

She expected Lady Hayward especially to argue with her about this point, but the lady simply placed a hand on Anna's arm.

"You cannot leave," Lord Comerfield said urgently as Anna forced herself to lift her head and look up at him, a little surprised to see such a great concern etched in his dark brown eyes as he searched her face. "It would make things all the worse for you should you retreat."

Anna shook her head, lifting her hands for a moment. "What does it matter?" she said hopelessly. "There will be many others like Lady Warwickshire and, no matter how many of your acquaintances you believe to be willing to support me, I shall never again have the freedom and the acceptance that was with me only a few days ago." Her chin lifted as she looked back at him steadily, an ache in her throat and her heart burning with sorrow. "It is entirely hopeless."

"No." His hand reached out and caught her wrist for just a moment. "No, Lady Anna, it will not be as you say. Lady Warwickshire may be one of a few who will refuse to listen but, I promise to you that I shall do all I can to have the *ton* hear the truth and reject the rumors. In time, you will find yourself in that place of freedom once more, I assure you."

Anna could not speak, for the touch of his hand to her wrist was sending all manner of emotions through her. She was instantly thrust back into that moment when he had caught her from behind, when he had pressed his cheek to hers, his lips close to her ear. She shuddered violently, and Lord Comerfield's eyes flared wide before he dropped her hand, stepping back just a little and lowering his head.

"Lord Comerfield is right to encourage you so, my dear," Lady Hayward said gently as the conversations around them once more began to increase. "Do not give up entirely based solely on the cruelty of Lady Warwickshire."

Turning her gaze to her companion, Anna let out a long sigh. "I am tired," she said as Lady Hayward smiled sympathetically. "I am tired of this all already. It would be much simpler to return home and allow these rumors to spread." She felt as though she were sinking into a sand pit that was continually pulling her down as though she had no energy left within her to fight and struggle against it.

"Pray, let me encourage you," Lord Rowley replied kindly. "Here, Lady Anna, take my arm. Accompany me to a few others whom I know for certain will not speak to you as Lady Warwickshire has done. That will lift your spirits, I am sure of it."

Anna looked at him hopelessly, seeing the kindness behind his words and yet feeling as though there was very little reason for her to do so.

"Please, Lady Anna," Lord Comerfield said gently. "And come the morrow, I should like to call upon you to discuss the situation further. To see if more can be done to assist you. To see whether or not there is any use in my presence alongside you if it is only to cause you difficulty."

Lady Hayward held up one hand. "Might I suggest, Lord Comerfield, that you do so at *my* residence rather than at the duke's," she said quietly. "Now, Lady Anna, why do you not do as Lord Rowley has suggested? There may be happiness here for you yet."

Anna wanted to shake her head and refuse, wanted to call for the carriage and have herself returned home immediately but, as she looked all about her and saw her sister, Lady Hayward, Lord Rowley, and Lord Comerfield looking at her expectantly, she knew she could not do such a thing. There was no escape at present, no matter how she herself felt. It seemed she was bound to this course for the present, even though she knew it would be entirely unrewarding.

With a tight smile, she took Lord Rowley's arm and allowed him to lead her away, even though Lady Hayward and Lady Selina followed after her. She did not look back, did not even send Lord Comerfield a single glance, but the gentleman himself could not seem to take his eyes from her.

CHAPTER SEVEN

Quite what had made him state that he would call upon Lady Anna tomorrow afternoon, Elias could not say. Had it been the desperate look in her eyes? The realization that she would not be given the same freedoms as before, despite his promise to do whatever he could for her? The way she had spoken, the hopelessness in her eyes, and the heaviness about her person had thrust a spear of guilt hard against his heart until he had found himself speaking with an eagerness he had not known was within him.

And yet, there was still a great deal of fear within him. Fear that he would be forced to wed Lady Anna despite his best efforts to change the situation for her. He did not want to have to do so, did not want to have his own situation changed simply for her sake, even though he knew full well he was entirely responsible for it. His urge to speak to her, to encourage her and to beg her to continue with his plan for a little longer came not only from a desire to have her restored to society, but also to make certain that his way of life could continue.

Is that being selfish? he wondered to himself as his carriage made its way towards Lady Hayward's town-house. *Or is that quite understandable?*

Wrestling with the question for a short time, Elias gave up trying to come to a decision as to whether or not his motivation was correct and, instead, chose to close his eyes and rest his head back against the squabs in the hope of calming himself just a little before he arrived. There was, he noted, a little anxiety playing about his heart at the thought of having to, once more, sit with Lady Anna and apologize profusely for what he had done. Was it that he did not wish to see her so sorrowful? Was the pain of his guilt too much for him to bear? His jaw worked as he recalled the way he had looked across the room last evening, only to see her standing there, her face white as milk and her eyes downcast. She had lowered her head, her hands clasped in front of her, and it was only then he had heard Lady Warwickshire speak.

He had acted without hesitation, breaking off his conversation with another lady without even a word of apology and making his way to her side so that he might defend her. It had done very little, unfortunately, given that Lady Warwickshire had been so very determined to believe everything that she had heard, yet he had found himself quietly glad that he had been able to step in to verbally set things to rights. He was quite certain that those who had listened to him, those who had been paying close attention despite the fact that they were not a part of the group, would have considered carefully what he had said.

"My lord?"

Elias opened his eyes only to realize that the carriage was now at a standstill, with the door open and a footman waiting for him to descend. A little embarrassed, he cleared his throat and climbed down quickly, looking up at the townhouse before him. Without hesitating, he hurried up the stone steps and made his way to the door, which was opened for him at once.

"Lord Comerfield," he said, handing the butler his hat and gloves. "I believe I am expected."

"You are, my lord," the butler replied, bowing. "This way, if you please."

The townhouse was very elegant in its décor, making Elias wonder if it was Lady Hayward's hand that had guided such decisions. Such thoughts distracted him from his true purpose until he came to the door of the drawing-room. Hearing his name announced by the butler, he stepped in after him and bowed low, giving him only a minute chance to see those within. When he lifted his head, he saw Lady Hayward standing tall, whilst Lady Anna finished her curtsy. Neither appeared to be welcoming and Elias dropped his head, clearing his throat as he did so.

"Please, do be seated, Lord Comerfield," Lady Hayward said, her voice a little cool. "You had no difficulty arriving here, I hope?"

"None whatsoever," he answered, sitting down stiffly into a straight-backed chair. "Might I ask how you fare today, Lady Anna?"

Lady Anna's gaze was not timid as he had expected, nor was it sorrowful. Instead, there was a glint in her eye that spoke of a deep anger, a tightness about her mouth that told him she was not at all contented. And he could not blame her.

"I am a little downhearted," she answered steadily. "Last evening, whilst I was grateful for Lord Rowley's assistance and, I suppose, for your intervention when it came to Lady Warwickshire, there did not come within me the surge of hope that all will be well."

Elias winced. "I am aware of that, Lady Anna," he replied hastily, "but it was only the first evening soiree and, as yet, I have not had the opportunity to speak to as many of my acquaintances as I would have liked."

She did not reply to this but rather continued to study him, her eyes searching his as though seeking to discover whether or not he spoke the truth.

"I have every intention to continue as I did last evening," he said, speaking with haste. "Lord Rowley is only the first of many, I assure you. And, besides this, you also have Lord and Lady Chesterton and Lord Stevenson, whom, I presume, must all believe you innocent. Lord Stevenson's betrothed, Miss Hemmingway, will, of course, also be glad to acquaint herself with you, I am sure of it." He gave her a small smile, but it was one she did not return. "We have just under three weeks remaining, Lady Anna," he finished, a little desperately. "Might you not be willing to continue with our endeavors until then?"

Lady Anna tilted her head and studied him, her green eyes glittering like emerald sapphires.

"It was only the very first occasion that we have attempted together," he finished, spreading his hands. "I am certain there will be more success, Lady Anna, if you would only be willing and courageous enough to pursue it."

Her lips twisted for a moment as her brow furrowed. "Do you intend to continue staying near me, Lord Comerfield, so that you might interrupt any conversation that does not please you?"

Heat infused his face as he heard the slight tone of scorn in his voice. "Would you have preferred me to remain silent, Lady Anna?" he asked, his words sharp and biting. "I did what I thought was best but, if you wish it, I can—"

"You must understand the difficulties you have placed upon Lady Anna," Lady Hayward interrupted before he and Lady Anna could begin to disagree all the more vehemently. "You said last evening there was more that might be done." She spread her hands. "Have you any further thoughts as to what such things could be?"

Elias began to stammer, scrambling for ideas as he searched the farthest recesses of his mind for any pertinent thoughts. He had quite forgotten that he had said such a thing to Lady Anna and certainly had not given any time to further consideration!

"I can see you have not," Lady Hayward answered, one eyebrow lifted as though she were not at all surprised. "However, I have done so and, as such, should like to place them before you now."

Elias nodded, a little taken aback but certainly more than willing to listen. "Please," he said, spreading his hands. "I should be glad to hear whatever you have to suggest, Lady Hayward." He dared a glance at Lady Anna, aware of how her lips turned downward, how her eyes were fixed to the floor rather than looking at himself or Lady Hayward. Evidently, she was less than eager to hear what Lady Hayward was to say, clearly still lost in a great deal of sorrow.

"We must organize a few specific events," Lady Hayward said briskly. "Whilst I am very grateful to Lady Chesterton for inviting Lady Anna to her evening assembly but, as we saw, there were those who were very dismissive of Lady Anna's presence. However, if we were to organize a few events where the guest list could be carefully chosen, making certain that those you consider open to accepting Lady Anna were greater in number than those who might not, then surely there is a greater chance of success?" She smiled brightly, and Elias felt his heart flood with hope. It sounded like both a plausible and a wise idea and, the more he allowed himself to consider it, the greater his delight became.

"That is an excellent suggestion, Lady Hayward," he said, as the lady's smile grew. "In doing so, we will be able to increase those willing to accept what is told to them about Lady Anna's innocence, until things are much improved." His gaze turned to Lady Anna. "What say you, Lady Anna?"

For some minutes, Lady Anna said nothing at all. Instead, she gazed at him fixedly, her face devoid of expression as she considered what had been said.

"It all seems most unfair, does it not?" she said eventually, her voice thin. "I am the one struggling to be accepted by society, whereas you, Lord Comerfield, appear to be returned to it without too much difficulty whatsoever!"

Elias' did not know how to respond. It *was* unjust, he had to admit, but that was how society worked. Gentlemen were given much more freedom and were pardoned much more easily than ladies of the *ton*. Even though he had admitted, time and again, that he had been the one at fault and that Lady Anna had done nothing wrong, the *ton* dismissed his mistakes and focused only on Lady Anna.

"I am sorry," he said, those words being spoken with genuineness. "I cannot answer your question, Lady Anna. But what I can do is assist you in this matter as best I can. Lady Hayward has made an excellent suggestion, and I am sure that such things can be organized relatively quickly. Lord Rowley intends to have a soiree very soon, I am sure, and Lord Stevenson spoke of throwing a ball." Leaning forward in his chair, he tried to speak with encouragement. "This approach might well succeed, Lady Anna. All I ask is that you search for the willingness and strength to move forward."

"And," Lady Hayward added quietly, "you ought not to avoid each other's company. To do so, as foolish as it might sound to say, will only add to the rumors that are being spread around London. It will be suitable for you to continue a quiet acquaintance so that the *ton* can see there is nothing between you both. To push yourself away from Lord Comerfield entirely, Lady Anna, would only increase the whispers."

"The agreement must come from you, however,"

Elias said with as much gentleness as he could. "I will not push this matter further unless you feel able to do so."

Silence reigned, and once more, tension began to build as Elias held Lady Anna's gaze and prayed that she would answer in the affirmative. It would be the answer to their difficulties, he was sure. It would bring Lady Anna back into society slowly, and certainly would remove any consideration of marriage between them!

"Lady Hayward." Lady Anna turned towards her chaperone, frowning slightly as she did so. "Might I ask if you would be willing to give me a few moments to speak with Lord Comerfield?"

Lady Hayward looked startled. "I do not think—"

"I will be quite all right," Lady Anna interrupted firmly. "It would only be for a moment."

Elias' heart began to pound as Lady Hayward rose from her chair and made for the door.

"A few minutes only, Lady Anna," she said firmly. "And the door remains open."

Lady Anna nodded but did not remove her gaze from Elias, who felt himself grow suddenly deeply uncomfortable with the situation. He was not certain what Lady Anna wanted and why she could not speak openly when Lady Hayward was present, and, to be truthful, he was a little afraid of what she would say.

"Lord Comerfield," Lady Anna began, her voice hard. "I can see that you are eager for what Lady Hayward has suggested to take place, but I must ask you something."

He spread his hands. "Please."

"You appear to be greatly concerned for me," she

said, rising from her chair and beginning to pace slowly up and down in front of him, no longer looking directly at him. "Might I ask, however, whether such a concern is *truly* for myself and for my return to society, or if it is solely for your own sake?"

Elias swallowed hard, feeling a dart strike hard at him. What was he to say? The truth? Or the lie that he believed would be best to say?

"You do not immediately answer," Lady Anna said coolly. "Is that because you are afraid of what I will say when the truth comes to light?"

"I confess that I think of myself as well as you, Lady Anna," Elias replied hastily. "But there is nothing wrong in that." Still feeling more than a little awkward, he pushed himself to his feet. "I do, of course, want you to recover from this, Lady Anna."

"Whilst making quite certain that nothing in particular changes for you," she retorted, her brows knitting together. "You are quite contented to make such a mistake and then continue on as you are. There is nothing for you that need alter. You will not reflect on this and then change your ways. What is to say that another young lady will not fall foul of your supposed 'mistakes' come the next time?"

Elias opened his mouth to respond, only to close it again as the coldness of her words began to wash over him slowly. It was as though each word had been a punch to his chest, for he blinked rapidly and attempted to catch his breath. He could not answer her, for everything she said was quite true. There was no guarantee that such a thing would not happen again for, whilst he had considered his behavior and had been regretful that he had behaved so foolishly, he had not decided he ought to change his ways. In fact, he had silently believed—although never spoken such a thing aloud—that by the time the following Season came around, he would be able to continue on just as he had been before this issue with Lady Anna had occurred.

She came towards him, her face pale and her eyes cold. Looking up at him, her face only a few inches away, she pressed one finger lightly against his chest.

"There is nothing within that heart save for yourself," she said softly. "You speak of a desire to help me, but within it is the hope that, when you succeed, your guilt will be assuaged, and you will be able to continue along your chosen path as you have always done." Her eyes held his, and the ice within her gaze ran straight through him, causing him to shiver. "So whilst I will accept your help, whilst I will do as Lady Hayward has suggested, I will do so in the full knowledge of your character—namely your selfishness and arrogance."

"Lady Anna," Elias replied, hoarsely, "I..." Nothing further came to mind, nothing more could be said. It was as though she had looked deep within his heart and had found the truth and pulled it out for all to see. He felt bare and vulnerable beneath her gaze, his whole body cold. Whether it was that he wanted to distract her, to end this chill that still lingered, or because of some other reason, he did not know, but before he could stop himself, Elias had reached up and caught her hand, pulling it away from his chest and holding tightly onto her fingers.

Shock poured into her expression immediately. Her

eyes flared, her color rose, and he heard her swift intake of breath. And yet, she did not pull her fingers away. Rather, she stood there and looked at him as though something had shifted between them, something that he could not quite make out himself.

There was a strange, flickering heat running through his hand now, up his arm and towards his heart. He tried to speak but found he could not, for no words came to his lips. The moment itself held such importance, and yet he could not explain, even to himself, as to why that should be.

"Lady Anna?"

She was gone from him in an instant. Her eyes darted to the door, her fingers wrenched out of his as she took a step to the side, looking past him towards the door.

"Lord Comerfield was just about to take his leave," he heard her say, turning slowly to see Lady Hayward looking at him curiously, her eyes searching his as though she could tell that something had occurred between himself and Lady Anna.

"Yes, yes," he said quickly, trying to set aside the flurry of sensations that still clambered through him. "I was. I was about to take my leave." Gathering himself quickly, he turned to Lady Anna and bowed, aware that she did not look at him but turned her head away as if to state that she could not even bring herself to face his direction. "I shall, Lady Hayward, make certain to speak to Lord Rowley at the very first opportunity, so that we can arrange for such occasions as you have suggested to be put in place." He tried to smile, fully aware of the curious look that still lingered in Lady Hayward's eyes. "I hope it will not be long before the first of these can take place."

"And in the meantime, Lady Anna, her sister, and I will attend whatever it is we are invited to," Lady Hayward replied, which brought a sharp glance from Lady Anna. "But I thank you for your willingness and your efforts, Lord Comerfield."

He bowed low, heat creeping up his spine and into his neck. "There is no need to thank me," he replied, recalling how Lady Anna had declared that there was nothing within his heart but himself. How little she must think of him now! "No need at all, Lady Hayward. This was my doing, and it is only fair that I should set it to rights." Lifting his head, he finally caught Lady Anna's eye. Her cheeks were still warm, but her brow furrowed and her lips pressed into a tight, thin line. "Good afternoon to you both."

CHAPTER EIGHT

"Are you quite prepared?"

Anna lifted her chin, turned, and gave herself a final glance in the mirror that hung on the wall above the mantlepiece. A calm, somewhat cold expression looked back at her. Her eyes did not sparkle with excitement as they had once done. There was no flush of anticipation in her cheeks. Rather, there was only a quiet expectation that this evening would be just as difficult as any other.

"I am," she said heavily, turning back to where Lady Hayward stood with Lady Selina. "Let us take our leave."

Rather than making her way to the door and expecting Anna to follow, Lady Hayward stepped forward and reached to take both of Anna's gloved hands in her own.

"You will not find as many trials present as before," she said, her eyes holding a firmness that Anna wanted to secure for herself but found that she could not. "It will be easier, my dear."

These last five days, Anna had attended every social occasion she had been invited to and had found each one a trial. There had been some who had greeted her, conversed with her, and treated her as though there had never been anything said about her, whereas others gave her the cut direct or turned their faces away whenever she came to join a conversation. One or two had made pointed comments, leaving Anna feeling utterly mortified and not at all welcome.

The only way she had managed to remain had been due to the support given by Lady Hayward, her sister, and, much to her displeasure, Lord Comerfield. He had made certain to stay near to her during such occasions and even though Anna bristled with indignance that society appeared to welcome him without any particular concern over his behavior—for, evidently, such things were expected of a gentleman—she had been forced to silently admit that he had been of help to her. If a comment was made within his hearing, he did not hesitate to come forward and speak directly to the person in question. Over and over, he had stated that she had not been the one at fault, that *he* had been entirely mistaken and utterly foolish, although whether those within the *ton* believed him, Anna could not say. It was a very awkward situation, for most who found themselves in such a scenario wed almost immediately so that the scandal was ended and rumors were dismissed, but it was not so for herself and Lord Comerfield.

Each evening, she had found herself very weary upon her return home. Yes, she had placed a smile on her face for the sake of her father and had told him that things were improving just a little when, in truth, she saw no progress whatsoever, but it seemed to keep the duke contented. That being said, he had warned her that there was now only a fortnight before a demand for marriage between herself and Lord Comerfield would be made, should she not be returned to society in much the same way as she had been before. Given that she certainly did not want to marry Lord Comerfield unless there was no other choice open to her, Anna had to pray that this new scheme of Lord Comerfield's would work well, even though she felt very little hope within her heart.

Sitting in the carriage as it made its way to Lord Rowley's townhouse, Anna took in a deep breath and closed her eyes, attempting to calm her growing nervousness. These last few days, she had found herself, inexplicably, thinking of the moment that Lord Comerfield had taken her hand back when she had been speaking to him alone in Lady Hayward's townhouse. There had been something incomprehensible in that moment, something that, even now, she could not fully understand. She had been so filled with anger and upset, torn apart by his lack of true consideration for her as she realized that he was just as keen to return to his old way of life without difficulty as he was for her to do so. She had not expected there to be such arrogance and selfishness but, upon seeing it, had felt her heart cry out painfully within her. When he had taken her hand, however, that agony had softened. The look in his eyes had been one of horror, of realization, as though he were desperate for her to remain silent so that he might consider what she had said. Heat had flared in her cheeks, her breathing had quickened, and, despite herself, she had not been able to pull her hand away.

Even now, thinking of it, she could not understand why she had been so transfixed. Being in Lord Comerfield's presence was a continual reminder of what he had taken from her and to have to admit, even to herself, that he was doing a good deal to help her was painful.

"We are arrived."

Lady Hayward's quiet voice pulled Anna from her thoughts, looking out of the carriage window to see Lord Rowley's townhouse just before her. Footmen were standing on the steps, ready to assist the guests inside, and, as she prepared herself, the carriage door opened, and a gentleman stood, ready to take her hand.

She gave it at once, believing it to be a footman, only to look down and see that it was Lord Comerfield.

Her breath hitched.

"I thought to wait to accompany you inside," he said quietly. "As I have said, Lady Anna, there will be many guests here this evening who will be glad of your company. There are some who will believe the rumors, of course, but I can assure you that they are in the minority."

She pulled her hand out of his the moment she stood safely on the pavement. "I thank you," she said tightly, not wanting to feel anything akin to what she had felt before. "There is really no need for you to wait, Lord Comerfield."

"It is not about any sort of requirement," he replied swiftly as Lady Selina and Lady Hayward joined them. "Rather, I wish to do so, Lady Anna. You have given me much to consider, and I must admit that your words have made their way into my heart and I find now that there is no way to remove them." His lips twisted, his expression hidden in shadow, given the flickering light of the lantern-lit street. "Much as I might wish to do so."

Anna did not know what response to give to such a statement, wondering whether or not she could believe his words. Were they spoken so that she might feel a little more sympathy for him? That she might not think so poorly of his character as she did at present? Or were they true, spoken with honesty and openness? She could not tell and nor, at this moment, did she wish to consider it any further.

"Shall we go inside?" she asked as Lady Hayward nodded and gestured for Lord Comerfield to lead the way. Anna's stomach swirled uneasily as she climbed the steps, the familiar anxiety that she now expected at social gatherings beginning to take hold of her again. Even the reassurances of Lady Hayward had done very little to relieve her of such fears, and with every step, Anna felt her heart begin to pound all the faster. Just what would this evening be like?

The welcome Lord Rowley gave her was, Anna had to admit, overly warm, but she could not pretend that she was not glad of it. Lord Rowley smiled and bowed and gave her all manner of reassurances that this evening would be more than delightful for her and, despite her agitation, she could not help but smile back at him and thank him for his generosity in hosting such an evening.

"You need not thank me," he said kindly. "I am more than glad to be of assistance to you at present. I may call myself a friend of Lord Comerfield, but that does not mean that I consider all that he does to be correct." A pained sigh left his lips, although she could see the twinkle in his eye. "And thus, I often find myself in the unenviable position of trying to assist Lord Comerfield in attempting to undo all the harm he has done, Lady Anna —although, in this case, the request is not at all problematic nor burdensome!"

A quiet laugh erupted from Anna's lips, chasing yet more of her anxiety away. "That is very generous of you to say, Lord Rowley."

He bowed. "Please," he said, gesturing towards the door. "I do hope that all goes well for you this evening."

Anna took a breath and followed Lady Hayward, the smile fading from her lips as she did so. Walking into the drawing-room, she felt her legs shaking terribly as a sense of weakness rushed through her frame. She was certain that, at any moment, someone would turn around to greet the new arrivals, only to look at her and then, in an instant, turn away again without hesitation. Being given the cut direct was deeply distressing should it only occur on one occasion, but, for Anna, it had happened so many times already, and she did not think she could bear more.

"Oh, good evening, Lady Anna!"

Her breath hitched, her chest tight and painful as she turned her head, afraid that it would be someone eager to speak to her only to make quite certain that she knew of their opinion of her. Instead, much to her relief, there stood Lady Chesterton, who had made her way directly towards her the moment she had come into the room.

"And to you also, Lady Selina, Lady Hayward," Lady Chesterton continued, ignoring Lord Comerfield entirely. "I am so glad to have been invited to this most *excellent* evening." She smiled warmly at Anna. "I am sure this will be a most enjoyable occasion for you, Lady Anna."

"I thank you, Lady Chesterton," Anna replied, surprised at just how steady her voice was. "It is very good to see you again."

Lady Chesterton smiled and then stood to the side, spreading one hand out to the rest of the crowd. "Should you like to come and join the conversation I was having with Lady Birkhill and Lord Westerton? I am sure they would be glad to have you all join them."

Anna's heart began to pound as she looked to Lady Hayward, who nodded and smiled, encouraging her to step forward.

"It will be quite well," she heard Lord Comerfield murmur behind her, his voice low and yet filled with such emphasis that she found herself wanting to believe him. "Go with her, Lady Anna."

Taking a deep breath, Anna made her way after Lady Chesterton, with both her sister and Lady Hayward following after them. Quite sure that, in a moment, Lord Westerton and Lady Birkhill would turn to look at them and then, after a moment, hurry away, she was more than a little astonished when the two guests turned towards Lady Chesterton and herself with warm smiles lighting their faces.

"Good evening, Lady Anna, Lady Selina, Lady Hayward," Lady Birkhill said with a bob of a curtsy. "And how do you fare this evening?"

Anna opened her mouth to speak but found herself a

little unsure of what to say. Lord Westerton and Lady Birkhill looked at her enquiringly, and heat flooded Anna's cheeks at the silence that followed as they waited for her answer.

"I—I am well," she stammered, flushing brilliantly. "And very glad to be here this evening."

"I am sure," Lord Westerton said with a knowing look in his eye. "I confess, Lady Anna, that I was one of the many in the *ton* who believed the rumors that were swirling about you. However, given that Lord Comerfield has spoken to me directly and, in addition, Lady Chesterton also, I feel as though I must beg for your forgiveness, Lady Anna." He grimaced. "It appears that society is much more inclined to pronounce guilt on the female sex rather than hold any accountability for the gentlemen."

Anna blinked rapidly, all the more embarrassed that tears had sprung to her eyes at Lord Westerton's words. Lord Comerfield had spoken to him, then? Had made it quite clear that she was not to blame in any way for what had occurred? She did not know what to say, and, much to her relief, it appeared that Lady Hayward knew precisely what it was she was feeling.

"That is both honest and very generous of you, Lord Westerton," she said, coming to stand by Anna. "And I must say, we are all very glad indeed to hear such words from you." Squeezing Anna's arm lightly, she gave everyone a bright smile. "Has the weather not been quite perfect these last few days?" she continued, changing the subject entirely. "It has allowed us to walk through the park almost every day!"

Anna managed to blink away her tears as Lady Chesterton quickly began to discuss the weather with Lady Hayward, finding her heart filled with relief and her whole being seeming to slowly relax and uncoil. Letting out her breath slowly, she turned her head to glance to her left and noticed, to her surprise, that Lord Comerfield was watching her from a short distance away. His brow lifted in silent question, clearly wanting to know whether all was going well. Anna found herself smiling, despite the fact that she did not even want to express anything to him. The look of relief on his face astonished her, surprised that he appeared to be so very concerned for her when she knew for certain that there was a good deal of selfishness in his motives. A gentle murmur from her sister drew her back towards the conversation and, for the moment, Lord Comerfield left her thoughts entirely.

~

"LADY ANNA."

Looking to her left, Anna turned slightly, freed from the conversation she had been having with Lord and Lady Raynham and leaving her sister and Lady Hayward to continue it without her.

"Lord Comerfield," she murmured, looking at him steadily. "Good evening."

His smile was small, his eyes searching hers. "The evening has been a successful one, I hope?" he asked as she looked at him carefully. "I have been watching as you spoke to various other guests." A small step took him a little closer to her and, for whatever reason, Anna felt her breath catch. "I do hope that you have not found any particular difficulties this evening?"

"I have found no difficulties whatsoever," she said honestly, a little astonished by the relief that immediately jumped into his eyes as well as the way he lowered his head for a moment, letting out his breath in a great huff as though he had been anxious to hear her answer. "I have also heard from some that you have been particularly diligent in informing them that I have had nothing whatsoever to do with the rumors that swirl through London because of your actions."

Nodding, Lord Comerfield lifted his head and looked at her again. "I have done what I can, Lady Anna, even though I fear it shall never be enough," he said heavily. "Some have listened to me, and some have not. But with Lady Chesterton present also, those who have been less than convinced have had her confirmation of my words." He spread his hands. "I do hope that, in time, things will continue to improve."

Anna's lips lifted of their own accord and she realized that, for the first time in some days, she actually felt happy. This evening had gone very well, indeed. She had not been shunned, she had not been thrust aside by anyone, had not been given the cut direct, and found herself enjoying the evening. "This has been wonderful," she found herself saying as though she could not remain silent, could not contain all that was in her heart even though she did not want to speak to him. "I have found myself happy this evening, Lord Comerfield."

The smile that split his face was one that brought a

brightness to his eyes, lifting his features entirely and, despite herself, Anna smiled back at him.

"I am so very glad to hear you say such a thing, Lady Anna," he answered, one hand pressed to his heart. "As I have said, I have considered what you have said about me. You have seen within my heart, Lady Anna, and have seen the truth of it." With a grimace, he shook his head. "You are correct. This situation is of my doing, and, thus far, I have done all I can to make certain that, whilst things improve for you, I *also* am kept from the consequences of my actions." Lifting his chin, he looked straight into her eyes. "But no longer, Lady Anna."

Anna frowned. "What do you mean?"

A small shrug lifted his shoulders. "I was against the thought of marriage, Lady Anna, but I am determined that, should it come to it, I will accept it without hesitation. In the meantime, I shall do everything I can to assist you, Lady Anna, by taking on the responsibility of ensuring that everyone in the *ton* is aware of my culpability." Determination flickered in his eyes, his jaw working hard for a moment. "I will repeatedly speak of my foolishness if I have to. I will tell of my shame over and over to those who refuse to accept it until they have no other choice but to do so."

"And, if that lowers your standing in society?" Anna found herself asking, reminding him silently that, thus far, very little had changed in terms of his reputation, given just how forgiving society was towards him. "What then?"

He spread his hands. "I hope for it, Lady Anna," he said in such a firm tone of voice that Anna felt herself almost immediately believing his words. "If it increases your standing, then I shall accept whatever consequences are brought to me." His hands felt to his sides. "I shall not continue on in such a way, Lady Anna. To behave as I have has brought such a difficulty for you that I cannot, in any good conscience, continue on as I have done. I shall not do so again, Lady Anna."

She did not know what to say, finding herself inclined to believe everything that he had said and a little surprised that he had been so open with her, particularly when they were in the middle of Lord Rowley's evening soiree!

"I do hope that things continue to improve, Lady Anna," he said, inclining his head in a small bow. "Good evening."

There was no opportunity for her to say more, for he left her side, leaving her watching him depart with a slow realization of just how quickly her heart was beating. Quite why it was doing so when she was not at all inclined towards Lord Comerfield and certainly thought very poorly of him, Anna could not say.

"He spoke to you, then?"

Lady Hayward's gentle voice captured Anna's attention and she turned her eyes away from Lord Comerfield to look at her chaperone. "He did," she answered. "I am... a little surprised as to what he said but—" She smiled. "It seems that this evening has been a success and for that, we are both very glad indeed."

"Not only he but I also," Lady Hayward told her, reaching to press Anna's hand for a moment. "I think that, as the very first of such an evening, it has been a very great success. If things continue, then I think that your prospects are good, Lady Anna."

Anna let out a long breath and smiled, looking at her chaperone and finding herself very grateful indeed for all that Lady Hayward had done.

"I thank you, Lady Hayward," she sighed, contentedly. "I must hope that it will all be as you say."

"It has gone very well, indeed, thus far."

Elias nodded, looking at Lord Rowley. "Thanks to you and to many others," he replied, a little grimly. "I do wish that I could do more."

Lord Rowley looked at him askance. "More?" he queried, lifting his brandy glass to him. "What else is it that you think you can do? You have already done very well indeed to escape from the prospect of marriage. What more is there to do?"

"I do not care about such a thing!" Elias practically threw himself from his chair, his arms akimbo. "I was concerned about it once, certainly, but now..." He did not finish his sentence but rather made his way to the window, looking out at the street below. "Lady Anna has made it quite clear that there are some characteristics within my heart that are less than desirable."

Lord Rowley snorted, clearly less than impressed with such a statement. "I hardly think that it is the first time such a thing has been said to you."

Letting out his breath slowly, Elias dropped his head. "Indeed," he muttered, running one hand through his hair. "I cannot pretend that what you have said is incorrect, Rowley, but for whatever reason..." Again, his words drew to a close before he could think of what to speak that would bring such a sentence to an end. He could not explain, even to himself, why Lady Anna's words continued to resonate with him. For whatever reason, he could not remove them from his mind. It had been almost ten days since Lord Rowley's evening soiree and still, he found himself continually considering Lady Anna and how she fared.

"You mean to say that because Lady Anna said such things to you, you have therefore decided to change your ways?" Lord Rowley asked, sounding quite astonished. "Even though I have told you, time and again, that behaving in such a flirtatious manner will, in the end, bring you nothing but difficulty?"

"And in that, you have been proven correct," Elias replied with a rueful smile. "But yes, I will confess that, for whatever reason, Lady Anna's words have lingered within my heart. I have been unable to set them aside, unable to simply dismiss them as I have been able to do with you."

Lord Rowley looked a little affronted at this but Elias did not take back his words nor apologize for what he has said. It was all quite true, and saying such things aloud was not something he felt any regret over. Sighing inwardly, he looked back out of the window and continued to wrestle with himself over his strange fascination with Lady Anna.

"Good gracious."

Turning his head to glance back at his friend, Elias saw Lord Rowley's eyes widening, his brows lifting.

"What is the matter?" Elias asked, turning himself towards his friend a little more. "Is something wrong?"

Lord Rowley shook his head but continued to stare at Elias, irritating him just a little.

"Well?" Elias demanded, spreading his hands. "What is it?"

Pushing himself to his feet, Lord Rowley took a few steps towards Elias, eyeing him carefully. "It could not be, Lord Comerfield, that you have finally come to *care* for someone other than yourself?"

Elias stared at his friend only to laugh aloud, shaking his head as though Lord Rowley was being utterly ridiculous.

"You deny it?"

"Of course, I do!" Elias exclaimed. "*You* are the one who is seeking a bride, are you not? I am not at all inclined towards such a thing."

"And yet," Lord Rowley pressed, "you say that you are no longer even *thinking* about your own concerns in this matter. Marriage to Lady Anna is not something that you feel you must avoid at all costs."

"That is because I am attempting to refrain from turning to my usual selfishness," Elias stated firmly. "Nothing more."

Lord Rowley continued to speak as though he had not even heard Elias' interruption.

"You say that her words have penetrated your very soul and, it is because of what she has seen within you, what she had shown you beyond any doubt, that you have found yourself eager to turn away from such behavior. Her welfare has finally become more important than your own, and, in considering her so, your heart has become involved."

Elias scoffed at this. "I hardly think so," he laughed, picking up his glass of brandy. "That is nonsensical."

"It is?" Lord Rowley asked, one brow raised. "You mean to suggest that there is no situation where what I have described could possibly be true?"

Elias opened his mouth to flatly deny any suggestion that he was taken up with Lady Anna, only to close it again as Lord Rowley continued to hold his gaze, his brow lifted still. He could not possibly be taken up with the lady, could he?

"I am quite certain," he said with as much seriousness as possible, "that my only concern for Lady Anna comes from the awareness of just how much difficulty my actions have brought her and, thus, what I now need to do thereafter in order to make certain that her future is restored as much as it can be."

"And you should no longer feel discontent if you were required to marry her?"

"Of course I should feel discontent!" Elias exclaimed, throwing up his hands and looking at his friend as though he were quite ridiculous. "You know I have no inclination towards marriage."

Lord Rowley said nothing to this particular remark, looking steadily at Elias as though he knew full well that he was not speaking the truth. Elias did not want to reveal it, however, for to speak so would only confirm to

Lord Rowley that yes, in fact, there was no particular discontent at the thought of matrimony to Lady Anna. These last ten days, he had managed to have many quiet conversations with the lady and, since she was now being slowly restored to society, had found her to be much more willing to speak to him at length without any evidence of the anger or pain that had been there previously. The thought of marriage to her no longer loomed before him like a great and ominous threat but had gentled somewhat, making him wonder whether or not it would have been such a grievous punishment.

"It means nothing," Elias stated, swiping the air with his hand as though he were bringing the matter to a close. "Lady Anna is being restored to society and, thus, I am slowly being freed from my responsibilities towards her."

"And you will be glad to see her receive attentions from other gentlemen?" Lord Rowley asked, one brow lifted. "You will not mind in the least should such a thing occur?"

"Not in the least," Elias replied without even a modicum of hesitation. "It is what she deserves, does she not? I should not be glad for her if she were to be forced into marriage with me, given that I am so lacking." These final few words, however, pushed something hot and painful into Elias' heart, making him grimace and drop his gaze. He had spoken such words aloud because they were exactly what he believed Lady Anna thought of him —lacking in every way required of a gentleman—and yet saying them with such levity did not bring the same lack of care to his heart. Instead, they prodded hard at him, bringing pain and frustration that he had not expected.

"Perhaps it is that you no longer wish yourself to be so lacking," Lord Rowley murmured as Elias turned away towards the window, tired of his friend being able to place his finger on precisely what was now troubling Elias. "Do you wish to be better so that Lady Anna might consider you?"

Elias closed his eyes and threw back the rest of his brandy. He was tired of talking, tired of the supposed consideration of his motivations and the innermost workings of his heart.

"Shall we make our way into town or are we to talk all afternoon?" he said brusquely, looking over his shoulder at Lord Rowley. "Hyde Park, mayhap? Or a walk through the busy streets of London?"

Lord Rowley grinned, irritating Elias all the more as he waited for his friend to respond.

"Very well, very well." Lord Rowley held up both hands, his palms out towards Elias. "I shall not continue in such a way any longer although, I shall say that I am very glad indeed to hear of what you have been considering, Comerfield. I think a change of heart is a very good thing indeed."

"I am sure you do," Elias replied dryly. "But that does not answer my question as to whether or not you wish to make your way into town this afternoon as we had planned?"

Lord Rowley chuckled, perhaps believing that Elias' eagerness to make his way into town came from nothing more than a desire to bring this particular conversation to a very conclusive end. "Yes, indeed," he said, after a moment. "Hyde Park would suit me very well, so long as we have time before the fashionable hour begins." His smile faded and his lip curled just a little. "I have no delight in making a state of myself upon Rotten Row."

"I hardly think you would do so," Elias replied as they both made their way towards the door. "Although I will agree with you that many a dandy has found themselves parading like a peacock upon that street!"

"Something neither of us are inclined to do, I am relieved to say," Lord Rowley replied darkly. "Thankfully, the young Miss Pettigrew has no inclination towards such a thing either."

Elias laughed. "Then Miss Pettigrew is still the object of your considerations at present?"

"She is," Lord Rowley replied quickly, surprising Elias with his fervor. "I have a great deal to consider when it comes to Miss Pettigrew, but I find myself quite taken with her thus far."

"I am well aware of that," Elias replied with a lop-sided grin as they both stepped out into the afternoon sunshine, ready to climb into the waiting carriage. "She does appear to be quite eager to consider you also." He was astonished to note the slight flush of color that came into Lord Rowley's face as they sat opposite each other in the carriage. Surely the man did not have any particular feelings for Miss Pettigrew. He had always thought that Lord Rowley would marry a lady that he considered to be well suited, rather than because of any emotions that might swirl between them!

"I am glad you think so, Comerfield," Lord Rowley answered, rapping on the roof. "I should not like to consider a young lady unless there was something within my heart for her. To find her suitable in both status and wealth is one thing, but to make certain that she is amiable, interesting and, to a certain extent, intriguing, is quite another." He smiled to himself and looked out of the window. "My wife, whomever she may turn out to be, will have captured my interest as well as my heart, for I do not think that a successful marriage can truly take place without such a thing."

Elias did not know what to say to such a statement, finding himself a little overwhelmed by the words that had come from Lord Rowley. Whilst he had known that his friend was pursuing marriage, he had never once believed that Lord Rowley would look for anything other than suitability from a young lady, but now, it seemed, he was quite wrong.

Unbidden, his thoughts returned to Lady Anna and, despite his desire to remove her from his mind, found that he could not. Lady Anna was practically perfect for any gentleman to wed, given that she was of high title and would have an excellent dowry and inheritance—and yet he had found himself shrinking from the idea of matrimony despite such accolades. And yet now, the more he came to know her, the more time they spent conversing—albeit the fact that they spoke of the improvements in her situation and the like—the less the prospect terrified him. Instead, it slowly improved itself upon him, telling him repeatedly that such a thing would be, in itself, a wonderful situation should it ever be required of him to accept it.

Elias frowned hard and lifted one hand to rub it lightly over his eyes. He need not think like that any longer. The situation with Lady Anna was improving, society was slowly beginning to pull her back towards their bosom, and, thus, his requirement for marriage was no longer as severe as it had once been. In a few days, he would have to go to the duke once more and speak to him about what had taken place, about the improvements that had been made, in the hope that the gentleman would permit him free of any such requirement to wed Lady Anna. That thought, that prospect ought to be of gladness to him, ought to fill him with relief and contentment, should make him breathe a sigh of great relief that such a thing would no longer be required of him. So why, then, did it plague his mind so?

"To be seen walking with me might not be wise, Lady Anna."

The lady turned her gaze to him and held it steadily. "I have been seen in your company often enough, Lord Comerfield," she answered, her green eyes catching the afternoon sunshine, vivid in their color. "We have attended many of the same occasions of late, have we not?" A small smile caught one side of her mouth. "We have stated that we shall not avoid each other for fear of spreading rumors further and, whilst I confess I believed Lady Hayward's suggestion to be a rather odd one, it appears that she has been right in her judgments."

Elias smiled and glanced at Lady Hayward, who was in conversation with Lord Rowley. "It did seem very peculiar that she insisted we continue on in a quiet acquaintance, Lady Anna," he agreed, "particularly when I am sure you had no wish to do so. But it does seem that she has been proven correct in her wisdom."

"That is precisely what I think," Lady Anna agreed firmly. "Lady Hayward has been more than wise, Lord Comerfield, and if she is happy for us all to walk together for a short time, then I will be glad to do so."

Glad? The word rang around his mind as he glanced at Lady Hayward, who immediately fell into step with Lord Rowley, leaving him to walk with Lady Anna. *Could she truly be glad of my company?*

He could not believe her to be so, not after what he had done. There was still a great deal of reconciliation to take place between them, still some restoration to occur between Lady Anna and the *beau monde,* but, thus far, all seemed to be improving.

"Your sister does not join you this afternoon?" he asked as they fell into step together. "She is not unwell, I hope?"

Lady Anna glanced at him. "She has a headache," she replied with a small lift of one shoulder. "I do hope that it will not increase in strength for I do know that she was eager to attend the ball this evening." Her lips turned downwards and she looked away, leaving Elias to surmise as to what might now be troubling the lady.

"I am sure that the ball will go very well indeed, Lady Anna," he said firmly. "The Earl and Countess of Wessex are always careful about their guest list for whatever events they choose to host. I am certain they would not have invited you without believing you to be quite innocent."

Lady Anna let out her breath slowly, her eyes darting towards his for a moment, only for her to then look away again. "It is the first social occasion I shall attend without the knowledge that it has been arranged carefully for my particular benefit," she said, a heaviness in her voice that he wanted to help lift from her. "It has almost been a fortnight since I have done such a thing, and I cannot help but fear it." Again, her eyes lifted to his. "Are you to be in attendance, also?"

He nodded. "I am," he said with a small, rueful smile. "The Earl of Wessex and I have known each other since we were boys, although I fear that his character is much better than mine! Our friendship, I am sure, is the only reason that I am invited to join them this evening, for as I have said, they do not usually invite rascals such as myself!"

This, much to his surprise, made Lady Anna laugh, and, when she did so, her face lit up completely. There was a fresh brightness in her eyes, a faint dusting of pink in her cheeks, and a happiness in her expression that made his heart lift with delight.

"Then I shall not need to fear that there will be others such as you present, Lord Comerfield," she said, lightly. "Although I do not believe that you intend to continue behaving as a 'rascal' might any longer?" One eyebrow lifted as she glanced at him, a few brown curls dancing at her temples as the breeze caught them for a moment. Elias swallowed hard, finding his heart quickening in his chest at the look in her eye, a heat rushing through him that he could not quite explain.

"N-no," he stammered, suddenly feeling a trifle

awkward without any real understanding as to why. "I have made a firm decision to no longer behave in such a manner, Lady Anna. I do hope that you are aware that such a decision has only come about because of you."

Her laugh, this time, was a little dry. "I believe what you mean to say, Lord Comerfield, is that it has come about because of the consequences that have followed for you as well as for myself, given what you chose to do."

"No, Lady Anna!"

The words flung from his mouth with such a firm exclamation that Lady Anna stopped dead, turning to look at him with her eyes open wide, astonishment blazing within her expression.

"Initially, yes," Elias told her, finding a desperate urge deep within him to tell her the truth of what he felt, to speak of the battle that now raged within his heart. "Yes, I confess that I was considering only my own self, that I thought only of the consequences that might follow should I have no other choice but to restore you to society in the traditional manner. In fighting to find another way, I fought solely for myself. But then I began to realize the true depths of the pain and the hurt that I had caused you. I saw the trials that you endured, the struggles that were forced upon you because of my selfishness. And then, Lady Anna, you spoke to me in such a way that realizations poured themselves into knives of steel and drove themselves into my heart with such force that I was quite overwhelmed."

Lady Anna dropped her head, turned, and began to walk once more, leaving Elias to hurry after her. He did not know what she made of such explanations but he continued to speak regardless, wanting to empty himself of the burden that had come upon him so suddenly, the burden to assure her that he was no longer that sort of gentleman.

"I have been unable to remove those knives from my heart ever since, Lady Anna," he continued, his tone now a good deal quieter, although his words still held a force. "In fact, I have discovered that I do not wish them gone. I wish them to linger so that I might be able to continue on through this life with a changed heart and an altered perspective. So whilst it may be correct for you to state that, at the first, my only consideration was for the consequences that might fall upon my own head, I can assure you that, for some time now, I have thought only of you."

Lady Anna kept her head low, her steps even but her hands clasped lightly in front of her as she walked. Elias felt heat sear his heart, rushing up through him into his neck as they continued to walk alongside each other, saying nothing further for some minutes. Perhaps he had been foolish to speak so openly. Mayhap he ought not to have done so, for mayhap Lady Anna did not want to hear such things from him. Ought he now to apologize for being so open? For speaking things he ought to have kept within himself?

"Lady Anna," he began, a little abruptly, "forgive me, I should not have—"

Her hand touched his arm, and Elias stopped at once, turning to look at her sharply. There was a small, gentle smile on her face as she kept her hand on his arm, silencing him all the more.

"No, Lord Comerfield, do not apologize," she said

softly, the touch of her fingers on his sleeve seeming to burn through the fabric and onto his skin. "You spoke well. It is only, I confess, that I find myself a little overwhelmed with all that you have said. I never once expected to hear such things from you, and to know that they are truly within your heart is something that has quite astonished me."

Without intending to, Elias found his hand settling over hers as though a gentle touch might convey his meaning all the more. "Each of my words and sentiments are true, Lady Anna," he said fervently as though he were a little afraid she would dismiss all that he had said without giving it any further thought. "I have no words of falsehood that are spoken only to please you."

She smiled at him, her expression devoid of any fear, any reluctance or disbelief. "And I trust every word, Lord Comerfield," she told him, as he gently lifted his hand, finding his heart swirling with a sense of relief. "I may not have done so some days ago, but thus far, you have proven yourself, and I cannot deny that." Her happiness was evident in her expression, and Elias found himself smiling back at her, his own contentment slowly being realized. "It may be that I shall never be as I once was within society, but I have enough acquaintances to hope that, perhaps next Season, I will be able to find a suitable match."

He frowned. "Next Season?"

Her smile faltered. "I do not think that such a thing is possible to accomplish this Season, Lord Comerfield," she answered honestly as Elias felt another stab of guilt slam through his heart. "But Lady Hayward believes that, by next Season, such a thing will have been mostly forgotten by the *ton* and that, therefore, I have a better chance of making a good match." She lifted one shoulder. "My father does not mind waiting another year, it seems, although I am sure he will say so himself when you next speak to him."

Elias swallowed hard as though the thought of Lady Anna being engaged to be wed was a troubling thought. It was not so, of course, for that was the aim of every young lady who came to London for the Season and, given that some gentlemen were also inclined towards such a thing, it was more than understandable that Lady Anna should seek matrimony. Why then did he feel as though someone had punched him, hard, in the stomach?

"Are you quite all right, Lord Comerfield?"

Lady Hayward's voice was bright and held a pinch of mirth as though she had seen something in his expression that was humorous. "You appear to be rather dumb-founded."

Gathering himself quickly—for he certainly did not want to explain anything to Lady Hayward about his innermost thoughts—Elias gave her a warm smile. "Indeed, I am quite well, Lady Hayward," he said as the lady and Lord Rowley came to join himself and Lady Anna. "It is only that, once more, I am reminded of my culpability when it comes to Lady Anna's difficulties."

Much to his surprise, a look of sympathy crossed her features. "But you have worked so very hard this last fort-night," she said kindly. "And Lady Anna has seen the fruit of it."

"But it might not have come about save for my foolishness," he said with a half-bow. "Would that I could undo such a thing."

"You are doing what you can to return Lady Anna to the position she held before," Lady Hayward replied, still speaking with such kindness that Elias wanted to hang his head, knowing all too well that he did not deserve it. "You have not hidden your acquaintance with Lady Anna and, therefore, have shown the *ton* that there is nothing other than that between you. With the soirees, the dinner parties, and the evening assemblies that have been organized specifically for Lady Anna's reintroduction to society—"

"And as well as your diligence in speaking to those who question things and making quite certain that they know the truth of your foolish actions," Lady Anna interrupted, gaining a quick look from Lady Hayward.

"All of these things have done a good deal to assist Lady Anna back into her place in society," Lady Hayward finished with a small smile that spoke of acceptance and, mayhap, even a little understanding. "I know that it was nothing more than foolishness on your part, Lord Comerfield. You did not mean to do as you did."

Lady Anna moved just a little closer to him and, his attention fixed to her in an instant, Elias turned his head to look into her eyes. She wore a grave expression, her gaze melding to his, her lips flat but without any anger evidenced within her.

"It was a mistake," she said. "A foolish mistake, certainly, but it was not done in bitterness or spite. I believe that, Lord Comerfield, truly. And," her lips pulled upwards, a small gleam coming into her eyes. "And if it is that such a thing has changed your character for the better, then that must also be a good thing."

Elias put one hand to his heart and bowed low, rather overwhelmed by the generosity that had been shown to him by both Lady Hayward and Lady Anna. "You are both much too kind," he said quietly, meaning every word. "I do not deserve any generosity, nor understanding, and yet you are willing to give both to me."

Lady Anna smiled as he rose, and he could not take his eyes from her. His concern for her had grown substantially over these last few days, and now, he was beginning to wonder if such concern would overflow into something more.

"We must return to the carriage," Lady Hayward said, breaking the quiet that had come between them for a few moments. "Our preparations for this evening will have to begin soon."

"I look forward to seeing you again tonight, Lady Anna," Elias found himself saying, garnering a look of astonishment from Lord Rowley. "I am sure that all will go very well indeed." He tilted his head to one side. "And if it does not, then I can assure you that I will do all I can to make it so for you."

"I thank you, Lord Comerfield," Lady Anna replied, giving him one more long look before she turned her attention to Lord Rowley. "Good afternoon, Lord Rowley."

"Good afternoon," Lord Rowley replied cheerfully. "Until we meet again this evening."

Lady Anna said nothing more but turned to walk back along the path towards her carriage, with Lady

Hayward quickly bidding both Elias and Lord Rowley farewell before hurrying after her charge. Elias watched them both depart, his brow furrowing hard as he attempted to work out what strange sensation it was this time that caused him to watch her so closely.

"Well, well," Lord Rowley murmured, dragging Elias' attention back towards him. "You had a pleasant conversation with Lady Anna, then?" He eyed Elias suspiciously as though everything he had seen and overheard now confirmed what he had always thought. "She appears to be much more inclined towards conversation with you."

"For which I am very glad," Elias replied, turning his back on the two departing ladies and making his way further along the path with Lord Rowley by his side. "It seems that her return to society is very near its conclusion. She is correct when she states that any thought of courtship or matrimony or the like will have to wait until next Season, however." His jaw worked for a moment, his brow furrowing hard. "I wish it were not so."

"There is a simple solution to such a thing," Lord Rowley replied with a sly smile. "Surely you can surmise what it might be without me having to explain such a thing to you?"

Elias rolled his eyes. "I do not think that the solution would be at all acceptable," he replied, knowing precisely what Lord Rowley spoke of. "The duke himself was glad that I should not wed his daughter," he stated with a lift of his brow. "To suggest it now would be—"

"But you are a changed man!" Lord Rowley cried as

though this was apparent for all to see. "It is not as though you are the scoundrel you once were!"

"I was never a scoundrel!" Elias protested as Lord Rowley began to laugh. "Now, enough nonsense. I shall not permit you to speak of such foolishness again!"

Lord Rowley chuckled and the two went on their way with jovial conversation. But, try as he might, Elias could not remove Lord Rowley's suggestion from his thoughts, even though, in his heart, he knew that such a thing could never be.

CHAPTER TEN

Anna smiled at her sister as they sat in the carriage. "You look much better, Selina. Have you recovered from your headache?"

"I am feeling much improved, I thank you," Lady Selina replied as Lady Hayward sat down and smoothed her skirts. "I hear that you walked with Lord Comerfield and Lord Rowley this afternoon."

Anna nodded but looked away. She did not want to speak of what Lord Comerfield had shared with her, for she had found her feelings towards him changing very rapidly these last few days. Having found herself to be very angry with him indeed, which had turned to frustration and upset, she had slowly begun to see just how much effort he had put into arranging events specifically so that she could be welcomed back into society without too much difficulty.

He had been present these last ten days. He had watched her carefully, had always been ready to step forward and speak to whoever he needed to, and, from what she understood, had lost some standing in society given what he had confessed to. By all accounts, he had made himself out to be worse than he truly was simply so that she might rise up in society's view, whilst he would sink all the lower.

"Lord Comerfield has been outstanding in his willingness to aid you, Lady Anna," Lady Hayward said quietly. "He will be here this evening, I understand."

"Yes, I believe so," Anna replied without any inflection in her voice. "As will Lord Rowley."

Lady Selina laughed. "Do not think that there is any opportunity for a connection to be made between myself and Lord Rowley," she said as Anna looked at her in surprise. "Although I could not say the same for you and Lord Comerfield."

An exclamation of astonishment left Anna's mouth. "I can hardly believe you have suggested such a thing!" she exclaimed as Lady Selina continued to laugh. "Such a thing is quite ridiculous. You know very well that Lady Hayward, Father, and I have concluded that *next* Season is to be the one where I shall find a match." She smiled sympathetically at her sister. "I am sorry that this has taken up so much of our time this Season, my dear sister. I know that you also have been seeking a match."

Lady Selina shook her head. "Have no concern for my sake," she replied warmly. "This situation is not of your doing and I have been glad to see things improving for you."

Relieved that she had managed to remove the subject of Lord Comerfield from the conversation, Anna lapsed into silence as the carriage made its way to Lord and

Lady Wessex's home. She did not even want to consider what had been said by Selina but try as she might, the thought whispered into her heart and refused to leave it. Would it be such a bad thing to wed Lord Comerfield? She had, initially, thought him nothing other than selfish and arrogant, unable to change in any way, only for him to prove her entirely mistaken. He *had* changed significantly. She had initially believed that he was attempting to encourage her back into society for his own sake rather than her own, but given how he had behaved these last few days, the way he had been ready and on hand to push as much of the blame onto himself as he could, had proved to her that there was far more consideration for her than before. And when he had spoken to her that afternoon, she had practically felt his desperation to prove to her that he had considered what she had said and allowed it to change him.

"Are you planning to remove yourself from the carriage or will you stay in there for the rest of the evening?"

Startled, Anna looked to her left and saw the smiling face of Lady Hayward looking back at her from the open door of the carriage. It seemed that both Lady Hayward and Lady Selina had not only climbed down from the carriage but had waited for her for some moments before evidently realizing that she was not even aware that the carriage had come to a stop.

"Oh, excuse me!" Anna exclaimed, making her way out of the carriage at once and grasping the hand of the waiting footman to help her climb down. "I was lost in thought."

Lady Hayward said nothing, although there came a knowing look in her eye as she smiled. Anna did not want to say anything of what she had been thinking and thus continued on her way up the steps to the entrance of the townhouse, her embarrassment at being so tardy blocking any sense of anxiety that came with attending the first of her social events in some time that had not had a carefully selected guest list. Welcomed by the hosts, Anna made her way into the ballroom with Lady Selina on one side and Lady Hayward on the other. Letting out a long breath, she gave herself a slight shake and lifted her chin.

"You will do very well," Lady Hayward murmured encouragingly. "Do not allow anyone to see should they affect you. But smile warmly, speak with spirit, and accept dances from those you choose without feeling at all inclined to accept every gentleman that approaches you."

"I will, Lady Hayward," Anna replied, taking in a steadying breath. "And thank you."

"I believe it is our dance, Lady Anna."

Anna looked up into the face of Lord Henderson, who had come to claim her for the waltz. She did not know him particularly well but, despite the advice of Lady Hayward, had found herself willing to accept any offers of dancing from any gentlemen who asked her.

"So it is, Lord Henderson," she replied, disliking the way the gentleman leered at her, his eyes a little dark. Perhaps she had been wrong to accept him, even though she knew him to be a gentleman. "If I might, Lady Hayward?"

Lady Hayward smiled and nodded, gesturing for her to take her leave with Lord Henderson. Stepping out onto the floor, Anna made her way to the dance floor on the arm of Lord Henderson. They said nothing at present, although he continued to glance down at her as though she were some sort of prized possession.

"You are doing rather well in society, it seems," he said as they bowed and curtsied to each other as the music began. "You have recovered somewhat."

"I have," she answered tightly, not at all appreciating his attempt to make conversation. Did he really think that she would want him to mention such a thing?

"And the rumors about your behavior with Lord Comerfield are quite untrue?" he asked, clasping her tightly around the waist and grasping her hand with the other. "I suppose they must be, given all that Lord Comerfield has been saying."

Anna fought down the flurry of embarrassment tinged with anger that began to burn in her heart. "There is no truth whatsoever, Lord Henderson," she replied stiffly, stumbling just for a moment, although Lord Henderson simply dragged her along with him until she was able to regain her footing. "I am very grateful to Lord Comerfield for making certain that the *ton* is aware of his actions."

Lord Henderson chuckled darkly as though such a statement was a very foolish thing indeed, as though he did not believe it to be true. Anna said nothing but continued to dance quietly, wishing that such a conversation was now quite at an end. But Lord Henderson showed no such eagerness, continuing to speak of all that had occurred with great relish and looking down at her keenly as though to surmise whether or not she herself had any enjoyment from it. Anna felt herself stiffen all the more and decided to remain utterly silent until the dance came to a close, no matter what Lord Henderson asked her. This was something of an impossible task, given just how much Lord Henderson asked, how much he demanded from her, and just how irritated he became when she would not speak of it.

"I will take from your silence, Lady Anna, that you are culpable in some way but do not wish to speak of it," he said as the dance came to a close. "That shall not make me think any less of you, however." He grinned at her as he bowed, his eyes holding a darkness that she did not much like. "I think a little more of you, in fact."

"If you would return me to Lady Hayward," she answered frostily. "I should be glad of it." She knew now that it had been a mistake to accept Lord Henderson's request for a dance, given all that he had said. His character was not a kind one, and she vowed silently not to be in his company again.

"This way, Lady Anna," he murmured, offering her his arm and, out of nothing more than requirement, Anna forced herself to take it. In the melee of couples leaving the dance floor, she did not realize that he was not returning her to Lady Hayward until it was much too late. Her heart began to pound as he led her through an open door and outside into the warm night air, attempting to wrench her hand from his arm but discovering, much to her fright, that his other hand was now tight upon hers, keeping it there firmly without her permission. Her heart began to pound furiously as he pulled her down the steps that led into the garden, and she knew she could not cry out for fear of being recognized. If she cried out, if she was seen by another, then they would know immediately who she was and the rumors that swirled around about her. Everything that had been pushed away from her, everything that she and Lord Comerfield had been trying to fight, would return to her tenfold. She would never again be able to hold her head up in society. Everything would come to an end.

But what else was she to do? If she lingered with Lord Henderson, then another guest might well see her and realize that she was out walking with him without a chaperone. But if she did not remove herself from him, then she feared what he would attempt to do! Would it be worse for her to hurry back inside alone, her chaperone entirely absent? Or to be discovered walking with Lord Henderson?

She did not have any further moments to consider for Lord Henderson, chuckling quietly to himself, pulled her into a darker part of the garden where they would not be seen.

"Unhand me!" she whispered furiously, her skin crawling with fear. "How dare you treat me in such a fashion?"

He laughed and let her hand go—and Anna made to step back at once only for him to grasp her tightly around the waist and pull her close.

"I do not believe a word of what Lord Comerfield has

been saying," he grated as she fought and clawed at his hands, trying to pull herself from him, but his grip was too strong and his determination much too fierce. "I think that you are more than willing to give a few affections here and there." Leaning closer, his breath ran across her cheek, and Anna shuddered, beginning to feel almost entirely helpless against his strength. "Or is it only to Lord Comerfield that you shall give them?"

"Let me go!" Anna cried, her voice no longer a whisper as she began to panic. "You should not have brought me here!"

Lord Henderson laughed again and made to lower his head but, just as he did so, something hard barreled into him from the side. Anna was released in an instant, staggering back as she fought to keep her balance. Her breathing was ragged, her hands pressed to her chest as she stared into the darkness, trying to work out what had just occurred. Her legs were trembling, her whole body shaking with fright until, finally, she heard a voice she recognized.

"How dare you!"

Lord Comerfield.

Anna closed her eyes, trying to breathe at a normal pace as she fought against the panic and fear that threatened to overwhelm her. She dared not move, she dared not step out into the ballroom now, not when she did not know what would be waiting for her. Had someone noticed her absence? Had they seen her being taken to the garden with Lord Henderson? If so, she dared not return, not when the guests would, once more, look at her as though she were the greatest of sinners.

"Lady Anna?"

Lord Comerfield's voice was quiet now, gentle and pleading as she looked all about her, her breathing ragged. "Lady Anna, please."

"I am here," she whispered, just as a figure came closer to her, making her jump violently. "Lord Comerfield?"

"I am sorry," he said, taking her hand and pressing it hard. "I did not think he would do such a thing and it took me some minutes to realize where you had gone."

Without having had any intention of doing such a thing, Anna found herself leaning into Lord Comerfield, her hands pressed against his chest as her head rested on his shoulder. She shook violently again and, after a moment, felt Lord Comerfield embrace her. It was not a touch that spoke of intimacy or any affection but rather gave her a great comfort that, for the moment, she so desperately needed.

"I will go and fetch Lady Hayward," he said gently. "Stay here, Lady Anna. Then you can return to the ballroom without any difficulty."

She shuddered again but pushed herself from him, nodding. "Has anyone within the ballroom noticed my absence?"

"I do not think so," he replied softly. "There are one or two others in the garden at present but, if you remain here and away from the path, then I am certain you will not be noticed." His hand pressed hers. "I am reluctant to leave you."

She closed her eyes and let out a long breath. "Where is Lord Henderson?"

Lord Comerfield's hand left hers. "He will not trouble you again," he said without giving her an answer. "I have made certain of it. I am sorry, Lady Anna."

She shook her head. "There is no need for you to apologize, Lord Comerfield," she whispered. "Now, if you please, might you go and fetch Lady Hayward? I am eager to return inside."

With a murmur of encouragement and a gentle touch of his hand, Lord Comerfield took his leave of her. Anna closed her eyes and tried to control her trembling, fully aware of the danger she was in. Should anyone discover her, then her reputation would be quite ruined.

Stay here.

The reassurance in Lord Comerfield's voice echoed back in her mind. He had been certain that she would not be discovered, that she would be kept quite safe should she only do as he asked. She had to trust him, even if it meant standing in a dark part of the gardens without any awareness of who was nearby or where Lord Henderson was.

The minutes seemed to stretch out into hours until Anna was not at all sure just how long she had been standing there alone. Her skin was cold, her fingers clammy as they wrapped around her arms, leaving her to shudder with both fear and the chill.

The sound of soft footsteps crossing the grass caught her ears, and she caught her breath, stepping back in fright—only to hear Lord Comerfield's voice.

"Lady Anna?"

She sagged with relief, one arm wrapped around her waist as she bent forward, dragging in air.

"Anna!" Lady Hayward was with her in a moment, her arms wrapped around Anna's shoulders as she pulled her close. "I was so afraid for you."

"She is safe," Lord Comerfield murmured, coming to join them both. "But we must hurry you inside, Lady Anna, before you are missed."

Anna dragged in air, looking into Lady Hayward's face and only barely able to make out her features. "I am sorry."

"There is *nothing* for you to apologize for," Lady Hayward said firmly. "Lord Comerfield told me he was not certain of Lord Henderson and watched him closely. He saw him lead you away from me, rather than towards me. I am very grateful indeed that he observed you with such a close eye."

"He would not let me go," Anna whispered hoarsely. "Lord Henderson said that he believed the rumors, believed that I would give him affections without hesitation. When I tried to push him away, he...he would have..." Her throat constricted and she sucked in air, feeling a little faint. "Lord Comerfield, had you not been present, then I fear what would have occurred."

"This is all entirely my doing," he replied grimly. "But come, Lady Anna, we must have you back inside very soon. The warmth of the ballroom will aid your recovery."

"And I will make certain that you do not leave my side for the rest of the evening," Lady Hayward answered, putting one arm around Anna's waist and beginning to walk back towards the path. "Claim a headache, if you must, but there is no requirement for you to dance with any other gentlemen if you do not wish it."

Anna swallowed hard but said nothing. Her steps were slow, her legs feeble as she climbed the steps, hearing the laughter, the music, and the joviality that came from the ballroom. When she was led inside, she winced at the noise, feeling it jar with the deep upset and shock that was contained within her.

"Look, there is none that stare at you," Lord Comerfield said as Lady Hayward led her to a quieter part of the ballroom. "None that whisper about you nor seem to have noticed your return. You are quite safe, Lady Anna."

Relief poured into her core, and she closed her eyes for a moment, coming to a stop as Lady Hayward stood by her.

"Here," Lord Comerfield murmured, handing her a glass of wine. "Have some, Lady Anna. It will restore you somewhat."

"And do sit down," Lady Hayward replied, guiding her into a chair "Lady Selina and Lord Rowley are dancing at present, but I am sure they will find us."

"I will go to meet them," Lord Comerfield interrupted with a swift nod of his head. "Excuse me."

Anna watched him go, feeling overwhelming gratitude for what he had done for her. The way he had watched her, the way he had realized that something was wrong, and the way that he had protected her from the cruelty of Lord Henderson. She took a sip of her wine and let the warmth spread through her, closing her eyes again as she began to quieten.

"I should never have let you—"

"There is nothing that you need apologize for, Lady Hayward," Anna said before her chaperone could say more. "Lord Henderson is a gentleman. I accepted his offer of a dance without question. Neither you nor I were to know of his motivations."

Lady Hayward wrung her hands, her expression one of despair. "But if something had occurred, then I do not know what I would have done."

Anna took another sip of her wine and then let out a long breath, feeling her shock begin to remove itself from her heart. "But it did not," she said softly. "Lord Comerfield was watching. He followed. He saved me."

"If only he had never made such a mistake in the first place!" Lady Hayward exclaimed with more wrath in her voice than Anna had ever heard before. "Then this might never have happened!"

"Or it might have occurred regardless, with another gentleman who thought they could steal a kiss or two from the daughter of a duke," Anna replied, strength returning to her. "I will not blame Lord Comerfield for this, Lady Hayward. It was Lord Henderson's doing entirely. Moreover, I am more than grateful to Lord Comerfield for what he did. Without his sharp eye, I fear that I would now have found myself in the deepest disgrace that could ever have been—and this time, it would not have been an accident on the part of the gentleman. It would have been entirely deliberate." She shuddered violently but did not default from what she was saying. "Lord Comerfield should be thanked, Lady Hayward, nothing more. Do not place blame upon his shoulders when it is entirely undeserved."

Her chaperone sighed and sat down in a chair beside her, clearly a little overcome herself. "You are quite right, of course," she said weakly. "It is only that I have been so overcome with the fright of hearing what he told me of your circumstance that I..." She shook her head. "I am grateful to him. But we must take a good deal more care, Lady Anna. There are those amongst the *beau monde* who will, it seems, seek to take advantage of you."

Anna did not answer. Instead, her eyes were fixed on Lord Comerfield, who was making his way back towards them with both Lady Selina and Lord Rowley with him. His expression was grim, his eyes set but his gaze trained upon her. Her heart lurched in her chest as he drew near, finding herself looking at him with respect and gratitude that had never been there before.

"Oh, Anna!"

Selina was beside her in a moment, her hand grasping Anna's as she bent to look into her face. "You are not harmed?"

"I am not," Anna replied, looking behind her sister to where Lord Comerfield stood, talking with Lord Rowley, who appeared just as shocked as her sister. "The sole reason being Lord Comerfield's watchfulness and devotion to my wellbeing." She caught his attention with her words, and he turned to look at her, his eyes holding a great deal of emotion, all swirled together as she looked up at him. "Might you call on me tomorrow, Lord Comerfield? I should like to discuss this evening in a little more depth—and to thank you for what you have done in a proper fashion."

He inclined his head. "There is no need for the latter,

Lady Anna, but yes, I should be glad to call upon you. I am only sorry that this evening has not been all that you had hoped."

A small sigh escaped her. "Aside from Lord Henderson, it has been an enjoyable evening," she admitted as Lord Comerfield smiled at her, his eyes brightening just a fraction. "But I look forward to speaking with you tomorrow, Lord Comerfield."

He bowed. "But of course, Lady Anna," he said, a trifle brusquely as though a little embarrassed to be speaking in such a manner when there were so many others nearby. "Tomorrow afternoon, then?"

She nodded. "Tomorrow afternoon."

CHAPTER ELEVEN

E lias cleared his throat for what was the third time and, with a lift of his chin, made his way to the front door. It was opened for him at once, and he stepped inside, refusing to give in to the urge to look over his shoulder for fear of who else might be watching him.

"Lord Comerfield," the butler said, appearing out of the shadows to bow before him. "The duke has requested that you speak to him before you call upon Lady Anna. If you would come this way, please."

After taking Elias' things and handing them to a footman to take care of, the butler led Elias towards the duke's study. It had not been a question as to whether or not Elias wished to speak to the duke but rather a demand that he do so—and Elias could not help but feel a little anxious.

The butler stepped inside, murmured something, and then removed himself from the room. With a nod of approval, he gestured for Elias to step through the open door, only to close the door tightly behind him the moment Elias had done so.

"Your Grace." Elias bowed low, wondering what it was that the duke wanted to say to him. "I am sorry that I have not arranged to come and speak to you these last few days. I am all too aware that the three weeks are almost past."

The duke waved a hand. "I am not here to berate you, Lord Comerfield," he said, gesturing him towards a chair. "In fact, I should like to speak to you about the situation at hand." Sitting down stiffly in a chair, he let out a small sigh before, much to Elias' relief, smiling at him. "I hear that you saved my daughter from a very dire situation last evening, Lord Comerfield."

"A situation of my making, Your Grace," Elias replied, only to see a dark cloud settle over the duke's features. "And by that, I mean that it would not have occurred in the first place had it not been for my foolishness. I did not have anything to do with Lord Henderson, of course."

The cloud cleared quickly. "I see," the duke murmured, tilting his head to the left. "All the same, that does not mean that I am not grateful to you for what you did. Lord Henderson is clearly a scoundrel and, if I could, I would call him out for it!" His brow furrowed hard, an angry look coming into his eyes as his lips thinned, but both the Duke and Elias knew that such a thing could not take place. Then the *ton*, who were thus far in blissful ignorance, would become fully aware that something untoward had occurred between Lord Henderson and Lady Anna.

"I wish I could have prevented him from stepping outside with her," Elias said honestly. "I am sure she was greatly distressed by all that occurred."

"But she was unharmed," the Duke said, emphasizing the last word. "And for that, you are entirely responsible. You may feel as though such a thing is your fault, Lord Comerfield, but such gentlemen will behave as they please and do as they wish regardless of what has been said about the lady by another." He eyed Elias carefully. "*You* have never behaved in such a way, I think?"

It was a question rather than a statement and Elias flushed, dropping his head for a moment. "I will state that I have never once done as Lord Henderson attempted to do last evening, Your Grace," he said honestly. "And I have no intention of ever doing such a thing either. In fact," he continued, lifting his head so that he could look into the Duke's face. "Your daughter has shown me the depths of my heart and I have found it severely lacking. I have, therefore, decided to change my ways entirely, although it is a little too late for Lady Anna."

The duke nodded, but there was a lightness about his expression that Elias had not expected.

"I am glad to hear you say such things, Lord Comerfield," he replied as Elias sat in his chair and wondered if their conversation would now come to a close. "We are also to discuss my daughter's future, I believe." Again, one eyebrow lifted and his eyes studied Elias with a scrutiny that made Elias wince inwardly. "You have sought to restore Anna to the *beau monde*. Lady Hayward has, of course, informed me of all you have done and the progress that has been made. I believe that my daughter is slowly being restored to society, but I do not think that she will find a suitable match until next Season."

A flurry of shame crept over Elias's heart. "Indeed, Your Grace," he said honestly. "And for that, I am deeply sorry."

"You have done all you can to make certain that there is no requirement for marriage between yourself and Lady Anna," the duke continued quietly. "Might I ask if such a thought still brings you great distress?"

Elias' eyes shot to the duke's. "Distress?" he repeated as though he wanted to make certain he had heard the duke correctly. "Your Grace, there is no distress within my heart when it comes to considering your daughter as a potential bride. As I have said, I have studied my heart, considered what Lady Anna has said of me, and have found myself severely lacking. Therefore, I have every intention of remaining as I am at present rather than returning to the gentleman I once was. However, whilst I would be glad to wed Lady Anna, to restore her fully to society in that way, I am quite certain that it would not be what she herself wishes for."

The duke nodded slowly. "You consider her feelings in this matter?"

"I consider her feelings in every matter," Elias replied fervently. "I owe her a great deal, Your Grace. I only want what is the very best for her."

"And you believe that matrimony would not be in her best interests."

Confused as to why the duke should ask him such a thing—for surely, the gentleman was still of the mind that Lady Anna should continue through society until she could find a suitable gentleman to court and wed her—Elias nodded slowly. "I believe that matrimony to someone such as myself would not be what she would desire," he said, slowly. "If, however, you found such a thing to be required, if you believed it to be the resolution to all of this, then I certainly would not refuse."

"You would treat my daughter well?"

Elias ran one hand over his eyes and shook his head. "Your Grace, I would do all I could to show Lady Anna just how much I appreciate her, consider her, and value her," he said, speaking openly and without hesitation. "I give you that assurance." He did not know what the duke intended by such questions, his heart beginning to quicken as he looked into the older man's eyes and saw the curious gleam within. Was he intending to order Lady Anna to wed Elias? Surely, he would not, not when there had been so much progress with the lady's return to society? Elias could not pretend that the thought of such a thing was not a welcome one, realizing slowly that he had come to care a very great deal for the lady over these last weeks. However, deep in his heart, he knew that it would not be what Lady Anna desired. She did not want to wed him. She wanted to make her own choice, to wait until the following Season so that she might return to the *beau monde* and find her own match. To force her into matrimony with him would only bring her more difficulty.

"Thank you for conversing with me, Lord Comerfield," the duke said, rising from his chair in an abrupt, hurried fashion and leaving Elias to stare at him for a moment in surprise before also scrambling to his feet. "I am grateful to you."

Elias blinked and nodded, bowing quickly. "But of course, Your Grace."

When he lifted his head, the duke was in front of him, one hand reaching out to settle on Elias' shoulder.

"Lady Hayward and I have had many a conversation about you, Lord Comerfield," he said gravely. "There is more in your heart for my daughter than I believe you are even willing to admit. I will not say that I have been convinced by your manner and am not at all certain that a match between you both would be for the best, but if it is something that Lady Anna herself wishes for, then I will not stand in her way."

Elias' mouth dropped open and it took him a few moments to gather himself. "Your Grace," he stammered, a little awkwardly. "As much as I care for your daughter, I would never put her in a position where she would be forced into a situation she did not want."

The duke nodded. "I am aware of that," he replied calmly. "As I have said, I believe that there has been a significant shift in your character, Lord Comerfield. Whether or not my daughter sees it, whether or not she considers you in a different light, is entirely up to her." He smiled suddenly and let go of Elias' shoulder. "But should you ask my permission, Lord Comerfield, I will give it to you."

Shock rippled over Elias as he stared after the duke, not at all certain what to say or what to do.

"You should make your way to the drawing-room," the duke said, waving a hand in a nonchalant fashion as though everything they had spoken of was entirely without consequence. "She will be waiting for you."

As though in a dream, Elias turned and made his way to the door, which was opened for him at once. Making his way through, he did not even turn his head to bid the duke farewell, all the more confused by what had just been said to him. Wed Lady Anna? Quite what Lady Hayward had said to the duke, he did not know, but evidently, it had been enough to convince the duke that Elias was a changed character. And so obviously changed that there was a suitability now between himself and Lady Anna that had not been there before.

Whether or not she considers you in a different light is entirely up to her.

Trying to follow after the butler to the drawing-room, Elias was forced to stop for a moment, his whole body burning with the realization of what was now before him. It seemed that, instead of simply assisting Lady Anna with the rest of her time in London, the possibility of matrimony was now before him. But was it something *she* might consider? Surely, she would want nothing more than to separate herself from him entirely, given all that he had done?

And you? said a quiet voice in his heart. *What is it that you wish for?*

There was not a single flicker of hesitation as Elias considered the question. He knew precisely what it was that he wanted. These last few weeks, he had seen Lady Anna begin to blossom back into a beautiful, confident young lady and had found himself desperate for her transformation to continue. He wanted to protect her, to encourage her, to support her, and to be near to her so that he might see her in all her beauty. There was more than just an eagerness to restore her to society within him now. There was a strength of feeling that he had not wanted to admit to himself, had not wanted to study for fear that he would realize precisely what it was. But it seemed that Lady Hayward had known of it, had known what was in the depths of his heart before even he had recognized it!

"But how am I to go about such a thing?" he groaned as the patient footman waited for him to continue on his way towards the drawing-room. He could not turn around and ask Lady Anna to wed him! Such a thing was quite preposterous. But if he did not, if he did not make his intentions clear as well as his reasons for doing so—affection rather than duty—then she would continue through society both this Season and the next until she found someone suitable to marry.

"Are you quite well, my lord?"

The footman was now coming back towards him, looking a little concerned, but Elias waved a hand. "I am quite well," he stated, giving himself a slight shake. "Please, lead on."

Straightening, Elias lifted his chin and told himself that such inner torment could wait until another time. He was to speak with Lady Anna this afternoon for a short time and, thereafter, attend an evening assembly. There would be time to think on what the duke himself had said later that evening, if not tomorrow. For the moment, he had to converse with Lady Anna for a short time.

His heart began to quicken at the thought of seeing

her again, following after the footman once more. It was foolishness, he told himself, nothing more than foolishness—but still, his heart pounded furiously as he was led into the drawing-room.

She rose at once, a beautiful smile on her face as she greeted him with a curtsy and a few words of welcome. His confusion and worry disappeared in a moment as Elias found himself smiling back at her, his eyes and his heart filled with none but her.

"Lord Comerfield, please do sit down," Lady Anna began as Elias hurried quickly to a chair, greeting Lady Hayward as he did so. "I am glad you are arrived."

"And how do you fare this afternoon?" he asked, looking at her anxiously as though he expected to find some great trauma etched across her features. "You are well?"

She smiled at him, and all of his fears disappeared in a moment. "I am much recovered," she said quietly. "That is why I wished you to call this afternoon, Lord Comerfield. I wanted very much to thank you for what you did last evening."

Lady Hayward murmured something about wondering why the maid had not yet brought the tea and, excusing herself, rose from her chair. Elias did not turn to watch her leave, although he was fully aware that Lady Hayward had left them both alone for a few moments. Quite why she had done so, he was not at all sure, although he had to admit there was a certain sense of anticipation growing within him now that she had done so.

"Lady Hayward will be back in a few moments,"

Lady Anna said, a faint blush capturing her cheeks. "She knows that I wish to speak to you alone."

"Oh?" Elias could not help but catch his breath as he attempted to remain just as calm as before, despite the pounding of his heart. What was it Lady Anna wished to say to him that could not be said in front of Lady Hayward?

"I must, as I have said, offer you my great thanks for what you did for me last evening, Lord Comerfield," Lady Anna said softly, her eyes lingering on his before she looked away for a moment, a faint blush rising in her cheeks. "Might I ask you why you were so intent on watching me last evening?"

Elias cleared his throat, feeling a faint swirl of embarrassment in his chest. "I watched you, Lady Anna, to make certain that you were treated well by those around you. You know that I have been willing to step in whenever I am needed, simply to make certain that the truth is well known."

Lady Anna nodded slowly. "You have been more than willing to do so and have been very diligent with it also," she answered quietly. "Might I ask, Lord Comerfield, if you intend to continue on in such a manner for the rest of the Season?"

"And for the next!" he exclaimed fervently. "I will continue to do all I can for you, Lady Anna, until you are settled and contented." Leaning forward in his chair, he held her gaze with a steadiness that spoke of the urgency and eagerness within his own heart. "I must know that my wrong towards you has not ruined your chances entirely, Lady Anna. I have to do what I can to make certain that your happiness can still be found."

She looked at him and then tilted her head in much the same manner as her father, her green eyes sparkling. "I believe I said to you some weeks ago that there was nothing but selfishness and arrogance within your heart, Lord Comerfield," she said quietly. "Now, however, I believe that such words would no longer be true."

"That is only because of you, Lady Anna," Elias replied quickly, wishing he could find a way to show her the depths of his heart without having to find the words to explain it. "Your pain was obvious to me, and guilt tore through my heart. But it lingered on my own self, on the consequences that I did not want to have to endure rather than focusing entirely on you. You saw such things within me and did not hesitate to reveal them to me, Lady Anna, and for that, I shall forever be grateful."

Her brows lifted in surprise. "Grateful?"

"Indeed," he replied eagerly. "Lord Rowley has often criticized me, but I have ignored him, believing myself to be quite contented just as I am. You, however, bore the consequences of my foolishness and your sharp words dug directly into my heart and forced me to consider my character as it truly is. What I found there was not as I had expected."

One corner of her mouth lifted. "No?" she asked softly, her gaze now gentle. "What did you discover?"

Elias spread his hands. "I found that all you had said was quite true, Lady Anna," he said honestly. "I was not as a gentleman ought to be. I was selfish. I was arrogant. And thus, in realizing such things and in seeing just how much pain and suffering I had brought to you because of it, I knew that I could not simply ignore such a thing. I had to do what I could to make certain that all manner of things within me changed for the better. I have found myself thinking of you and what you said so many times, Lady Anna. I pray now that such a change is evident within me."

Lady Anna's expression softened all the more. "It is," she answered, filling his heart with such a great surge of hope that he did not know what to make of it. "It is so very wonderful to see, Lord Comerfield. And after last evening, I am all the more grateful to you for your willingness to continue watching over the interactions I have with others. That, I think, speaks of the...consideration that you have for me at present. Although, I do not want to become a burden to you, Lord Comerfield." Her brow furrowed and her gaze flickered as she glanced away for a moment before lifting her head to look at him again.

Elias was out of his chair before he could stop himself. "You are not a burden to me, Lady Anna," he said with such fervor that he felt the truth of it fill his chest, wanting desperately to explain to her all that he felt and yet knowing he could not. Instead, he hunkered down before her as though he were a subject and she his royal queen. "I do not consider your company nor my responsibility towards you to be a burden. Rather, I accept it gladly. It is precisely because of you that I have found myself so changed, and, in that, I am truly grateful." Aware of the urge to reach out and take her hand in his, Elias rose to his feet and refused to give in to such thoughts. "It is not just consideration for you that fills my heart, Lady Anna," he finished, still looking down at her and seeing the way her eyes held to his, an expression of deep curiosity held within them. "It is more that I have come to care for you."

The words rang around the room with such force that Elias felt them strike hard at his chest, but he did not say anything more, refusing to pull them back. They were the truth, and he did not want to hide from the truth. Lady Anna's eyes grew wide with astonishment, her mouth opening just a little as though she wanted to reply but could not find a way to do so. Elias smiled at her and then, turning, made his way back to his seat, hearing Lady Hayward's footsteps coming to join them.

"The maid is just about to bring the refreshments," she said glibly, although Elias was quite certain Lady Hayward knew very well that words of great importance had been shared between both himself and Lady Anna in her absence. "She had thought you still with the duke, Lord Comerfield."

Elias smiled at her. "There is no particular urgency," he said, sitting back comfortably in his chair and finding, much to his surprise, that he felt less burdened than before. In speaking as he had to Lady Anna, there was no longer that deep sense of urgency within him, urgency to tell her of what he felt. He had said enough, had told her enough for her to realize the truth of what was within his heart and, for the present, that would satisfy him.

"And you are to attend the evening assembly tonight?" Lady Hayward asked as Elias nodded. "Another excellent evening, I hope!"

"I am sure it will be," Elias agreed, daring a glance at

Lady Anna and seeing that her cheeks were now blossoming with color, her eyes darting between himself and Lady Hayward. A small smile crossed his face as a sense of satisfaction and relief flooded him. "Yes, Lady Hayward. I am certain it will be an excellent evening indeed."

Anna looked down at her dance card. "The country dance," she murmured, looking back at Lord Hillock. "You are very kind, Lord Hillock. I look forward to it."

The gentleman beamed and then turned to Lady Selina, requesting her dance card also. This particular evening assembly had only a few dances but Anna was being very careful indeed as to who she gave them to. There was to be none of the carelessness that had come with the previous ball, not when she had found herself in such a difficult position with Lord Henderson! Her breath hitched as she recalled just how Lord Comerfield had come to her aid, how he had held her close in the gardens, reassuring her and comforting her for a few moments before he had gone in search of Lady Hayward. If anything had proven to her that he was not the gentleman he had once been, *that* had been the moment. He had not sought to kiss her, to encourage her towards intimate affections with him. She had been very weak and overcome with shock and he had done nothing but offer her his support and aid. No, he was not the gentleman she had once thought him to be. The change in his character, the way he watched and considered her, were all entirely genuine, and Anna was very happy indeed to see it.

I have come to care for you.

Those words had not left her ever since Lord Comerfield had spoken them. It was foolish of her, of course, to let such sentiment linger on within her heart, but she could not rid herself of it. It was as though something had ignited itself within her, something that she simply could not let go of within her own heart. Part of her wanted to question Lord Comerfield further, wanted to know precisely what he had meant by such words, but another part of her wanted nothing more than to refrain from such an action, fearing what it might then lead to.

"You are very quiet this evening."

Anna turned to see Lady Hayward smiling at her and, with a small shrug, tried to let out a small laugh.

"I am a little distracted, that is all," she said, hoping her chaperone had not overheard what Lord Comerfield had said that afternoon. "I am being very careful indeed with the company I choose for myself, however."

Lady Hayward smiled. "I am glad of it," she said softly. "And did your conversation with Lord Comerfield go as you had hoped? I know you wanted to discuss the matter of Lord Henderson without interruption so that you might speak openly." Her eyes searched Anna's face. "Did that occur?"

Anna nodded tersely. "It did," she said, quickly, not

willing at all to mention anything further. "I thank you, Lady Hayward, for your understanding."

Lady Hayward chuckled. "I do not think your father would have approved of me stepping out for so long, but I well understand the need to speak about such a matter without being overheard," she said, reaching out to squeeze Anna's hand for a moment. "Although, if there is anything that you wish to speak of, anything that you might wish to discuss further, then you know that I am more than willing to listen and offer what little advice I have."

Anna opened her mouth to say that there was nothing more she needed to discuss, but closed it silently, refraining from comment. She was, she realized, having very odd feelings towards Lord Comerfield and that, certainly, was something that she needed to think on a little more before she could make any sense of it.

"No?" Lady Hayward murmured, a twinkle in her eye. "Perhaps not yet, then."

A flush caught Anna's cheeks. "Not yet," she replied, a little embarrassed. "I am not even certain that there will be anything at all to discuss, Lady Hayward!"

"But it is about Lord Comerfield, is it not?" Lady Hayward asked gently, turning to face Anna a little more. "I have spoken to your father about the possibility that there may yet be a match between you."

Astonished, Anna stared at her chaperone, who only smiled back at her with a kindness in her expression that Anna knew came from the very depths of Lady Hayward's heart.

"I have seen the way he has come to care for you,"

Lady Hayward continued, quietly. "I know that his change in character is of great significance to you, even if you are yet uncertain as to how to move forward with such awareness."

Anna closed her eyes, hearing Lord Hillock laugh as he continued in conversation with her sister. "I do not know what has come over me," she said reluctantly as though she did not truly wish to speak to Lady Hayward but found herself unable to remain silent. "I find that Lord Comerfield's actions, his consideration of me, and his continued determination to only seek my best for me has had a profound effect on my heart."

"Indeed, as it well might," Lady Hayward replied gently. "I know that you were angry with him—and rightly so—but what he has done thereafter speaks highly of his change in character."

"But can I be certain of it?" Anna asked aloud, the question appearing on her lips even though she had never once thought it within her mind. "Is his change in character to be considered a permanent change?"

Lady Hayward pondered this for a moment, then lifted one hand. "I cannot say, Lady Anna," she replied gently. "I would not guide you in this matter either, whether or not I had my own opinion. Such a thing must be your own choice, your own decision. Speak with Lord Comerfield if you wish, for I am sure that he has his own feelings on the matter." The twinkle in her eye returned and Anna could not help but laugh.

"If you are as aware of things as you state, then I am sure that, by now, you are fully aware that Lord Comerfield has more than just a general consideration for my wellbeing, Lady Hayward," she said as her chaperone laughed softly. "But yes, you are quite correct." Becoming a little more thoughtful, she nodded to herself. "I will consider things further and decide what it is I shall do. Initially, I had thought I would wait until next Season to find a suitable match, but…" She trailed off, frowning hard for a moment, her gaze settling upon Lord Comerfield who had only just entered the room. Had her eyes been drawn to him? Had something within her known that he was about to come into the room?

"But if there is a match waiting for you here already, a match where you might find happiness and respect—if not something more—then why wait until next Season?" Lady Hayward asked, turning to see where Anna was looking. A little embarrassed, Anna dropped her gaze and turned her head away from Lord Comerfield.

"Indeed," she said, heat rising up within her. "Or perhaps I am being foolish."

"That will be for you to decide," Lady Hayward replied firmly. "But now, look. You are to dance with Lord Stockbridge, are you not? Here, he is about to approach."

Distracted from her thoughts with the prospect of dancing with Lord Stockbridge, Anna quickly placed a smile on her face and turned to greet him.

∼

"Good evening, Lord Bowman. Thank you for the wonderful dance."

Anna curtsied quickly just as Lord Bowman bowed towards her.

"My pleasure," he replied with a warm smile. "I look forward to dancing with you again, Lady Anna."

Anna smiled and nodded, watching him depart with a warmth growing steadily within her heart. It seemed that her return to society was, in fact, improving with every day that passed. The evening assembly was not an event that had been organized by Lord Comerfield, and nor had it a carefully chosen guest list, but thus far, she had not found any particular difficulties. Yes, there were one or two ladies who turned away from her, and one in particular had given her the cut direct, but Anna had not felt the sting of it as badly as she once had. Thanks to Lord Comerfield's endeavors, she had found herself very happy indeed this evening and prayed silently that such a success would continue.

And then next year, you can return and secure a match, she reminded herself, looking vaguely around the large room and wondering who she was next to dance with. *Unless there is something else that you might consider first.*

Closing her eyes, Anna took in a steadying breath and gave herself a slight shake. She had been overcome by these strange emotions ever since Lord Comerfield had come to her rescue, and, to her astonishment, they had only increased since then. There was no reason for her to have such strong feelings, but they simply would not leave her. She wanted to look for him, to speak to him, and to, in some way, confirm for herself whether or not this change in character was true.

Her breath hitched. Lord Comerfield was leading a young lady from the dance floor. His expression was a little grim, and there was not even a flicker of joy in his eyes. The young lady, however, appeared to be talking excitedly and at great length, looking up at Lord Comerfield earnestly. He stopped and turned to her, bowing his head, only for the lady to reach out and catch his arm.

Anna's heart began to pound. It was clear what the young lady was hoping for, was perhaps asking for, and the question now remained as to whether or not he would indulge in such a request. She watched closely as Lord Comerfield shook his head and turned away, only for the young lady to follow him. Anna's brow lowered as she watched the actions of Lord Comerfield, wondering where the young lady's mother or chaperone had gone.

And then, they stepped out of her view.

Agonized, Anna took a small step forward to look after them but saw nothing. Where had they gone? Her heart screamed at her to discover the truth, to go after them and find out what was occurring as though she needed to know precisely what actions he would now take. It would prove to her whether or not this supposed transformation of his character was genuine.

"I—I must go to the retiring room," Anna murmured just as Lady Hayward looked at her. "Might I be excused for a moment?"

Lady Hayward nodded. "We will wait here," she said as Anna began to step away. "Do be careful."

Anna gave her chaperone a quick smile and made her way in the direction of the retiring room, which, to her knowledge, was through the door to her right. There was no sign of Lord Comerfield and the young lady, making Anna's anxiety begin to increase rapidly. She desperately prayed that he would not be accepting her affections, that the truth of his declaration that he was a changed man would be proven correct.

"The retiring room?" she inquired of a footman, who directed her through the door and then to turn again to her right. Anna nodded, turned her head to see Lady Hayward still watching her, easily able to see where she entered, before making her way through.

The hallway was quiet and empty. There were two doors, one on either side of her, with the rest of the large hallway before her for a short distance until it split to the right and left, no doubt leading to other grand rooms. Anna frowned. If Lord Comerfield was not here, then where had he gone?

Her heart sank, and she lowered her head, reaching out one hand to press it against the wall for a moment. There was nothing about this situation that was good. It seemed that Lord Comerfield and this particular young lady had disappeared, and she had no need to question what it was they had gone to do.

"Enough!"

The exclamation caught her ears, startling her as she looked ahead of her, having just been about to step into the retiring room. Her heart began to thump furiously in her chest as she took a few small steps forward, wondering what it was she would discover should she reach the end of the hallway and turn the corner. She heard a quiet laugh, and the sound tore at her, making her fear what sight she would soon behold.

"I do not ask for your company, Miss Johnson."

"But you have it."

Anna closed her eyes as she lingered in the shadows, hearing the conversation but having no willingness to step out to see the situation with Lord Comerfield and this young lady. Dread filled her. It had been foolish of her, then, to even consider Lord Comerfield in such a fashion. Evidently, he could not resist the attentions of a young lady.

"The *ton* is full of whispers about you, Lord Comerfield," she heard the young lady say. "Why should I not take advantage of it?"

"Because I do not wish for it!" he exclaimed as Anna's eyes flew open, wide with astonishment. "You should not have followed me here. Your mother is waiting."

The young lady laughed again, a shrill, free laugh that spoke of no sense of consideration for anyone other than herself. "She does not care where I have gone! So long as I have the very best of company."

Shaking her head, Anna turned her face away, relief filling her. It seemed that Lord Comerfield was not doing as she had expected of him. A sense of shame crept over her heart, and she squeezed her eyes shut tightly. Lord Comerfield was not pursuing the lady, was not accepting what she offered. Rather, he was pushing her as far from him as possible, but, for whatever reason, this Miss Johnson simply would not depart from him.

"Enough, Miss Johnson!" Lord Comerfield's exclamation was louder than before, and Anna looked over her shoulder fearfully, worried that another guest would make their way through the door and hear the conversation. What would happen then?

"I do not care if we are caught," came Miss Johnson's quiet purr. "For then what shall you do, Lord Comerfield?" She laughed again, and the sound made Anna shudder. "You will have no other choice but to consider me your bride, and what harm can there be in that?"

"I shall never marry you," came the hard reply. "I shall not permit you to fix this situation in such a way that benefits you only." A gruff mutter came after this statement as though Lord Comerfield was attempting to move away from the lady but was being prevented from doing so. Anna frowned. Just what was Miss Johnson doing?

"There can be no harm in a few stolen moments," Miss Johnson crooned as though speaking to a very small child and evidently choosing not to continue with the subject of marriage. "What difficulties can there be in accepting what I offer you?"

"I do not want your affections!" Lord Comerfield replied harshly. "I do not want *any* affections! Can you not understand that?"

There was a hard silence, and Anna's heart quickened to such a rapid pace that she had to gasp for breath. She knew that she ought to return to Lady Hayward, knew that she could well be discovered by another guest at any time, but simply could not remove herself from where she stood.

"You care for someone else," she heard Miss Johnson murmur, sounding more than a little astonished. "Can it be true?"

"My affections are none of your business, Miss Johnson," Lord Comerfield growled. "Unhand me and remove yourself from my company at once. I have no time for this or for you."

His words were hard, and Anna found herself stepping forward, making her way around the corner only to see Lord Comerfield pressed back against the wall with Miss Johnson standing directly in front of him with only an inch or so between them. Lord Comerfield was unable to move without bodily removing Miss Johnson, and clearly, he had no wish to do such a thing for fear of any repercussions. As she stood there, the many candles illuminating her presence, she saw the flicker of fear that immediately tore into Lord Comerfield's eyes.

"Miss Johnson, is it not?" she said crisply. "Do allow me to accompany you back to your mother. I am sure that, by now, she is waiting for your return, as is my own chaperone, Lady Hayward." She stepped forward and took hold of Miss Johnson's arm, who, evidently overcome by great astonishment, allowed Anna to pull her away from Lord Comerfield." Anna shot a quick glance towards Lord Comerfield, seeing how he remained precisely where he was as though he required the strength of the wall just to keep him standing. His eyes were wide with shock, his face appearing a little pale, and he did not even attempt to speak.

"Excuse us both, Lord Comerfield," Anna continued, fighting the urge to rail at Miss Johnson and to shake her senseless also. Grasping Miss Johnson's arm tightly, she propelled her back towards the door with the young lady saying nothing and seeming to sense Anna's anger.

"You shall not achieve what you so desperately hoped

for, Miss Johnson," Anna said as the footman opened the door for them. "Lord Comerfield has refused you, and I shall say nothing of this matter." Triumphant, she looked at the young lady steadily and saw the flicker of a frown that crossed her face—but she did not care. "Return to your mother, Miss Johnson, before you bring any further embarrassment to yourself."

She let the young lady's arm go, and for some moments, the two looked hard at each other. For a second, Anna believed that Miss Johnson might simply turn around and make her way back towards Lord Comerfield again, but, should she do so, Anna had no qualms about following after her once more. This determination must have been evident in her expression, for Miss Johnson's shoulders sagged, her eyes dropped to the floor, and she turned at once to make her way across the room, back towards her less-than-responsible mother.

Anna let out a sigh of satisfaction, which, soon after was accompanied by a delighted smile of joy. Lord Comerfield had proven to her—albeit entirely without intention—that he *was* just as he seemed. His character *was* changed, and, from what she had heard, he had no intention of returning to such a way again.

Setting her shoulders, Anna considered for a moment whether or not she was to return to Lady Hayward or to do as her heart wished and make her way back to Lord Comerfield. The shock in his expression had torn at her heart, and she wanted now to reassure him that all was well, that she had overheard everything and knew precisely what he had done. But she knew that her responsibility was to Lady Hayward. Hoping that the gentleman would seek her out himself, she reluctantly made her way back to her chaperone who had been watching for her carefully.

"Who was that young lady?" Lady Hayward asked as Anna rejoined her and Lady Selina. "The one you stepped out with?"

"A Miss Johnson," Anna replied a trifle grimly. "But I do not think that such an acquaintance is worth pursuing, Lady Hayward, for she is not the sort of creature I should wish to call a friend."

Lady Hayward looked as though she wanted to say more, only to be interrupted by the arrival of Lord Hillock. In a few moments, Anna was back on the dance floor with Lord Hillock by her side, although her thoughts remained entirely upon Lord Comerfield.

She could hardly wait to see him again.

Elias was utterly miserable. Everything, he was sure, was at an end. Having only just discovered an affection within his heart for Lady Anna, he had now been ruined by the arrival of Miss Johnson. He had never expected her to follow after him when he had set her aside after their dance. He had never once expected to turn the corner of the long hallway as he sought the card room, only to find her thrusting herself against him, desperate, it seemed, for him to accept her affections.

The appearance of Lady Anna had made an untenable situation all the worse. His heart had failed him, overcome with shock and dismay. He had not known what to make of her actions, for she had practically pulled Miss Johnson away from him, and, evidently also in the depths of astonishment, the lady had gone with her without hesitation.

Making his way through the busy London streets, Elias hunched his shoulders against the cold wind. The weather, it seemed, also felt his misery for it had decided to take a turn for the worse. No longer was it beautiful sunshine, for dark clouds had gathered, and a chilly wind had begun to blow. He did not know why he had come out into London when he was so very downhearted but he had spent the last two days in his house, refusing to see anyone and unwilling to make his way out to any social events, and he had felt as though he ought to get a little fresh air.

It is hopeless, he told himself as he pushed open the door to a bookshop and stepped inside. His spirits were low, his heart aching with the realization that all was at an end between himself and Lady Anna, even though none of what had occurred had been his doing.

"Good afternoon, my lord."

Barely giving a nod of recognition to the proprietor, Elias made his way to the very back of the bookshop, wondering for the second time why he had decided to make his way into town.

"Oh, Lord Comerfield! How glad I am to see you!"

His heart slammed hard into his chest as he looked up to see none other than Lady Anna standing before him. She held a book in her hand, but upon her face was nothing more than a wide smile, her eyes alight with evident happiness.

"Lady...Lady Anna," he spluttered, astonished by her presence. "I did not expect—"

She reached out and settled a hand on his arm, her smile fading slightly as she held his gaze. "You have not come to call upon me," she said quietly. "I have been waiting for a note to arrive from you, or for you simply to appear! Why have you not done so?"

He stared at her, astonished by the question as well as her evident eagerness to have his prolonged company. "I do not understand," he replied slowly. "You saw me with Miss Johnson."

Lady Anna's expression softened, and a gentle smile tipped the corner of her mouth. "Lord Comerfield, I overheard your conversation with Miss Johnson," she told him. "Every word."

Elias blinked rapidly, trying to catch his breath as the significance of what she had revealed to him finally hit home.

"Then you know," he breathed, "that I had nothing but reluctance when it came to her desire to..." he could not finish his sentence, more than a little embarrassed already.

She laughed softly. "Yes, I am more than aware," she said sweetly. "I am sorry that I could not find you thereafter to tell you so myself, but given that it was an evening assembly, I had to dance and converse and could not leave Lady Hayward to go in search of you." She frowned for a moment. "You did not leave, I hope?"

"I did," he replied, remembering to keep his voice low so that he would not disturb the quietness of the shop. "I could not bear it, Lady Anna. After the look on your face, I was certain that you thought so very poorly of me. That you could no longer believe that anything I had said, anything I had told you, could bear any sort of truth."

Her hand slipped down to touch his, and a thrill ran up Elias' spine. "I am sorry for your distress," she said softly, taking a small step closer to him. "I thought that you would have known I had heard everything since I took Miss Johnson from you. She said she did not care if she was seen, knowing that to be discovered in such a compromising position would demand marriage at once—and I could not allow that to happen to you, Lord Comerfield, not when you have already given so much." Something flickered in her eyes, and she dropped her head. "I confess that I saw you and Miss Johnson as you left the dance floor," she said quietly. "I wanted to know that I could trust your words, Lord Comerfield. It would not be true to pretend that I just happened upon you."

Awareness dawned. "You followed me?"

Her head lifted, but her eyes were clear. "I am glad I did," she stated, her fingers pressing his. "I know for certain that you are a gentleman of changed character. I can trust you without hesitation."

Elias did not know what to say. His heart was pounding furiously, his mind overwhelmed with thoughts and emotions. The urge to step forward and to pull her into his arms, to hold her close and whisper the truths of his heart, was almost overpowering, but, with an effort, he did not.

"Lady Anna," he said quietly, trying to find a way to put words to all that he felt. "I have been broken-hearted these last few days, fearing that I have lost your company forever. And in that time, I have come to realize that there is more to our acquaintance than I have felt with any other."

Her smile was one of encouragement, and Elias found himself eager to continue.

"I have spoken to your father," he said, garnering a look of surprise from the lady. "He states that he would not be against any further...intimacy between us, Lady Anna."

"Lord Comerfield," she said quickly before he could say anything more. "Speak to me clearly, if you will. I must know what it is you are trying to say, for my own heart is quickening at such a rapid pace that I fear, very soon, this place will echo with the sound of it!"

Elias could hardly believe his ears. Here stood the lady that he had found himself gradually coming to care for more than he had ever cared for any other, only to believe that he had lost her entirely. Now, it seemed that she felt something akin to what was within his own heart —and he dropped his head, passing one hand over his eyes as he did so.

"I do not deserve any kindness from you, Lady Anna," he said softly. "It has been a revelation to me to realize just how much I have come to care for you. Indeed, I have been unable to think of anything else but you these last few weeks. I now realize, Lady Anna, that the prospect of marriage is not one that I turn from. Instead, it is one that, when I consider it, brings me nothing but joy."

Lady Anna remained silent for a moment, looking up at him as she considered. "When you draped yourself over me in your drunken state, Lord Comerfield, I never thought for a moment that I should ever find my heart softening towards you," she said as Elias ran his thumb over the back of her hand. "I believed you callous. Selfish."

"I was," he answered without any intent to deny it. "I was both, if not more."

Her lips twisted, her eyes a little dim. "I held a great deal of anger towards you, Lord Comerfield. I was lost and confused, hurt and fearful that I should never again be able to return to society. But as the days passed and I became aware of your actions more and more, those feelings slowly began to dissipate and were soon replaced with something more."

Elias swallowed hard, still struggling to take in all that was occurring.

"You showed me that your consideration of me came before anything else," she continued quietly, again moving just a little closer to him. "That selfishness faded from you. You put all of your efforts into making certain that I was the one being considered, rather than yourself. There was not an opportunity wasted, for you continually and repeatedly took the blame upon yourself and told everyone the truth of what you had done. No doubt, you have slipped farther in the *ton*'s considerations, but that means nothing to you, it seems."

"It does not," he rasped, her nearness overwhelming his senses. "The only person I have come to care for, Lady Anna, is you."

Her smile filled his heart. "And it seems, Lord Comerfield," she said softly, "that my heart speaks the very same."

Elias stood quietly with her for some minutes, simply looking down into her eyes and finding such a sense of joyous contentment that he did not want to move from it, did not want to let it be taken from him. The possibility of matrimony, the one thing he had been so afraid of from the first, now loomed before him like a great and delightful reward that he knew he did not deserve and yet he reached for it with every fiber of his being.

"I should like to court you, Lady Anna," he said, eventually, as her eyes brightened. "I have such a great affection for you. I cannot turn my face from you, for you have become of such importance to me. The first strains of love are within my heart, Lady Anna, and I am certain that they will only grow all the more, should you be willing to accept me."

She laughed and blushed furiously as he lifted her hand to his lips and kissed the back of it, lingering there for a moment. This was all so new for him and yet so wonderful. He only hoped she felt the same.

"Lord Comerfield," Lady Anna murmured, her free hand reaching up to press lightly against his chest. "My heart sings with joy at what you have asked me. I cannot refuse you, not when the love you speak of is within me also." Her smile was bright, her eyes sparkling with happiness, and still, Elias could not quite believe that such a thing was occurring. It felt as though he were in a dream, the most wonderful dream he had ever had in his life.

"My dear Lady Anna," he replied as she laughed up into his face. "I swear to you that I shall never betray your trust. That I shall give my all to you, that I will never step away from you. For you have stolen my heart entirely, and it can never be given to anyone but you."

. . .

I am glad Lord Comerfield and Lady Anna finally realized they were meant for each other! Please check out the first book in the Landon House series, Mistaken for a Rake. A sneak peek is available just a few pages ahead!

Already read Mistaken for a Rake? How about A Rogue for a Lady?

Saved by the Scoundrel
Mending the Duke
The Baron's Malady

The Returned Lords of Grosvenor Square
The Returned Lords of Grosvenor Square: A Regency
Romance Boxset
The Waiting Bride
The Long Return
The Duke's Saving Grace
A New Home for the Duke

The Spinsters Guild
A New Beginning
The Disgraced Bride
A Gentleman's Revenge
A Foolish Wager
A Lord Undone

Convenient Arrangements
A Broken Betrothal
In Search of Love
Wed in Disgrace
Betrayal and Lies
A Past to Forget
Engaged to a Friend

Landon House
Mistaken for a Rake

Christmas Stories

Love and Christmas Wishes: Three Regency Romance
Novellas
A Family for Christmas
Mistletoe Magic: A Regency Romance
Home for Christmas Series Page

Happy Reading!

All my love,

Rose

A SNEAK PEEK OF
MISTAKEN FOR A RAKE

CHAPTER ONE

"Do hurry up, Rebecca! The carriage has been waiting for some minutes and you are, again, tardy."

Rebecca bit her lip and forced herself not to retort words she would later regret back to her father. She would have liked to have told him the reason she was a little later than he expected was that she had spent some time sorting out a strong disagreement between her twin sisters, Anna and Selina. That had been a very lengthy discussion, and thus, she had been left with very little time of her own to prepare for this afternoon's outing.

"The carriage, the carriage!" the Duke said, ushering her in. "Your sisters are waiting!"

Smoothing her skirts as she sat, Rebecca looked at her sisters enquiringly, seeing the blush on both of their faces. They knew full well that the duke had been irritated with her when the fault was entirely their own. Of course, neither of them confessed, given that their father was already irritated and they did not want to incur his wrath.

A little frustrated, Rebecca turned her eyes to the window, hearing her father give instructions to the driver before he climbed into the carriage. She took a breath, letting it out slowly, dampening down her frustration.

"Now that we are *quite* ready," the Duke said, the door closed behind him, "perhaps we can finally be on our way to Madame Bernadotte." He sighed heavily. "You will have to be much more punctual from now on, Rebecca. From what I recall of London society, it is not at all acceptable to be late to soirees and dinner parties."

"Yes, Father," Rebecca replied monotonously. There was no excitement within her at the prospect of being a part of London society. Instead, there was the heavy burden of knowing that, most likely, she would have to guide her younger sisters through London in the hope that they would find suitable matches, for her father certainly would not do so. These last few years, her father had become more and more detached from his children, and Rebecca had been the one to step in where her father had failed.

Nothing would change now that they were in London, she was sure of it. He would expect her to do as she had always done. What hope did she have of finding a husband for herself when she had the responsibility of her twin sisters? It was just as well that the younger three remained at the estate in the care of their governess, else Rebecca did not know how she would have managed even to step outside the house!

"Rebecca?"

Turning her attention back to her father, Rebecca tried to smile. "Yes, Father?"

"Make sure that your sisters find what they require," he said vaguely. "I have no notion of fashion plates and the like. They will be guided by you."

Sighing inwardly and wishing that she knew what the fashion was to be this Season, she gave her father a brief nod and then returned her gaze to the window. This was going to be a very difficult Season indeed.

"Oh, I beg your pardon!"

Rebecca stumbled back, heat pouring into her cheeks as she realized that she had practically walked into another lady of the *ton* without realizing it. "Are you quite all right?"

The lady laughed and put one hand out towards Rebecca. "You need not worry, my dear," she said kindly, her blue eyes sparkling. "Are you going to Madame Bernadotte's?" She gestured to the establishment just ahead of Rebecca, her smile warm and friendly.

"Yes, yes, I am," Rebecca replied, still a little embarrassed. "My father..." She closed her eyes, then opened them, taking in a deep breath. "Forgive me." Dropping into a quick curtsy, she smiled back at the older lady. "If you would permit me to introduce myself, I am Lady Rebecca. My father is the Duke of Landon. He is presently inside with my two sisters, Lady Anna and Lady Selina."

"I see," the lady replied. "Then I do not think we should keep a duke waiting, Lady Rebecca. Shall we?"

A little surprised by the lady's forwardness, Rebecca

nodded and turned towards the door, all the more astonished when the lady followed after her.

"My son, it seems, has purchased me a pair of most expensive gloves," the lady continued with a wry smile. "He and I have come to London to speak to my late husband's solicitors about a few affairs. I think this gift is to encourage me to remain in London a little longer!"

Rebecca turned her head, lowering her voice as they walked inside. "I am sorry to hear of your husband's passing."

The lady smiled sadly, her expression now a little morose. "It was some years ago, Lady Rebecca, but I miss him still." She sighed softly, then gave herself a small shake. "But my son, the new Lord Hayward, has done very well in taking things on at the estate."

"I am glad to hear it," Rebecca replied, still feeling a trifle uncomfortable about the amount the lady was sharing when they had not been formally introduced. "I should go in search of my sisters now."

The lady's expression brightened. "But of course. Are you to have new gowns from Madame Bernadotte?"

Without meaning to, Rebecca allowed a heavy sigh to escape her, which, seeing the astonished look on Lady Hayward's face, only made a blush color her cheeks.

"Forgive me," she stammered, aware of her father's rumbling tones coming closer to her. "I did not mean to make any expression of complaint, Lady Hayward. It is only that, given that my mother is no longer with us, I have been given the responsibility of ensuring that my sisters and I are dressed appropriately. If I am truthful, I do not know precisely what would be best." She shrugged, heat still pouring into her face. "We have never been to London, and I do not know much about society." Quite why she was expressing this much to a lady she had never met before in her life, Rebecca could not explain, but there was something in the lady's expression that was so welcoming and encouraging that she felt as though she could tell her anything.

Lady Hayward tilted her head, her eyes considering. "I would be happy to assist you in this, Lady Rebecca," she said slowly. "I am aware that we have only just met, but if you have no other friends within London as yet to aid you, then I would be glad to offer my assistance."

"Assistance?"

Rebecca closed her eyes briefly, hearing the note of confusion in her father's voice.

"Father," she said quickly, turning to face the duke and seeing how his green eyes—so akin to her own—were watching Lady Hayward with something like suspicion. "This is Lady Hayward. She and I were quickly introduced as we came into this establishment. She is, very kindly, offering to do what she can to ensure that my sisters and I choose gowns of the highest fashion." Smiling quickly, she gestured to Lady Hayward. "Lady Hayward, forgive my improper manner. I should have introduced you properly." Praying that the lady did not think her entirely unsuitable for being anywhere near London, she tried again. "Might I present my father, the Duke of Landon."

Lady Hayward curtsied quickly, although she did not show any sign of awe or astonishment at being in the presence of a duke, as Rebecca had seen so many visitors do when they had come to the estate. "Good afternoon, Your Grace. I am very glad to meet you. As Lady Rebecca had just informed you, I would be glad to assist her with the ordering of suitable gowns for this Season." She smiled, and Rebecca saw the way the frown began to lift from her father's face. "In truth, it can be quite a burdensome task!"

Rebecca held her breath for a few moments, looking towards her father and entirely uncertain as to what his reaction might be. She prayed that he would be willing to permit Lady Hayward to do as she had offered for, whilst Rebecca had only just met the lady, she was certain that any assistance she could receive at this present juncture would be most appreciated.

The duke harrumphed for a moment, his gaze turning towards Rebecca, who continued to watch him hopefully.

"Very well," he said, speaking slowly as though he was not quite certain that such a thing was appropriate, his brow furrowing as he looked back towards Lady Hayward. "But only if it does not delay you, Lady Hayward."

Lady Hayward laughed and shook her head. "No, it does not," she replied with a smile. "In truth, I would be glad for the distraction! I have very little else to occupy me at present." Turning her head, she smiled at Rebecca, who, with relief, smiled back. "Might you introduce me to your sisters, Lady Rebecca? I should be glad to meet them."

"But of course," Rebecca said quickly, putting one

hand on her father's arm. "Father, if you wish to wait, then might I suggest—"

"I would be glad to chaperone your daughters, Your Grace, if that would be of assistance."

Rebecca stared at Lady Hayward as she not only interrupted Rebecca but spoke with such a boldness that Rebecca herself was caught by surprise.

"As I have said, I have nothing else to occupy me at present and choosing gowns can take many hours," Lady Hayward continued, her eyes dancing as the duke's frown deepened at the obvious displeasure that came with knowing he would be forced to remain at Madame Bernadotte's for some time. "My carriage is only just outside, and I would be glad to return them to the house when we are finished here."

"How very good of you, Lady Hayward," the duke said, inclining his head just a little. "I confess that I am somewhat out of my depth when it comes to what my daughters require." His eyes studied the lady for a few seconds before he nodded. "It would be a great help to me if you would do as you have suggested, Lady Hayward. That would mean that I could continue with particular matters of business that require my attention." A slight narrowing of his eyes betrayed his flickering uncertainty. "But are you quite certain that you have nothing else to occupy you this afternoon? I should not like to take advantage."

Rebecca feared that Lady Hayward would take offense at this clear disbelief, for it was more than apparent that the Duke was not at all certain that Lady

Hayward spoke the truth, but much to her relief, the lady in question did not appear at all perturbed.

"Your Grace, as I was telling your daughter only a few minutes before, my son, Lord Hayward, has purchased me a pair of gloves from Madame Bernadotte's, which I am now to collect. Thereafter, I have nothing at all to engage me for, like you, my son has matters of business to attend to."

"And you have no daughters?"

"I do," Lady Hayward replied, her expression gentling as she thought of the young lady, "but she is not yet out and remains at the estate. I am here in London with my eldest son in the hope of resolving a few matters of business. I will return home soon, of course, but not before such things are settled."

Hearing the two voices of her sisters echoing through the establishment, Rebecca turned a pleading gaze towards her father. "Might I take Lady Hayward to my sisters, Father?" she asked, but the Duke did not so much as glance at her. Rather, he fixed his gaze upon Lady Hayward, his eyes thoughtful as a look of interest drew into his expression.

"You are very kind to offer such a thing, Lady Hayward," he said slowly, choosing each word with care. "I would be in your debt, should you be willing to bring my daughters home once their gowns have been ordered. However, I wonder if I might, thereafter, ask if you would be willing to speak with me at greater length once you have returned them to the house." He looked at the lady steadily, and a swirl of anxiety swept through Rebecca's frame. What was it her father was doing? And what was it he wanted? She could not imagine what he intended to say to Lady Hayward, and, from the way the smile was beginning to fade from Lady Hayward's expression, it seemed that she could not either.

"If you wish it, Your Grace," Lady Hayward replied, a line forming between her brows as she watched the Duke, seemingly intent on deriving his wishes a little better by studying him. "I will, of course, do as you ask."

The Duke smiled suddenly, a light coming into his eyes that had not been there before. It was as though Lady Hayward's agreement had brought a sense of delight to him, although still, Rebecca did not know what to make of it all.

"Excellent, excellent!" the duke exclaimed before turning back to Rebecca, one hand on her shoulder. "Now, Rebecca, you shall make certain that your sisters behave with all propriety. They must make an excellent impression here in London, even within the dressmaker's!"

"Yes, Father," Rebecca murmured, her gaze sliding towards Lady Hayward, who was, she noted, watching the Duke with interest. "I will, of course, do as you ask."

"Wonderful," the Duke replied, seemingly now very relieved that he would be freed of the burden of his daughters. "I shall return to the townhouse, then. Make certain to do all that Lady Hayward asks and listen to her advice." His hand lifted from her shoulder, but the familiar weight of responsibility immediately came. "And, of course, there is no need to concern yourself with the cost of such gowns, Rebecca. Choose whatever you wish and whatever is needed and have the bill sent directly."

"Yes, Father," Rebecca murmured, dropping her head as warmth entered her cheeks. She wished he would not speak of his wealth in such terms, not when Lady Hayward was present. It was, she considered, a little uncouth and ill-considered but, given that her father was not likely to listen to any word she had to say on the matter, Rebecca remained entirely silent.

"Capital!" the Duke boomed before bidding a quick farewell to both Rebecca and Lady Hayward and then making his way to the door. A tight band released itself slowly from Rebecca's chest as she heard the bell tinkle above the door of the shop, signaling that her father had left. A small sigh left her lips as she looked at Lady Hayward, who was watching her with a good deal of curiosity.

"I should introduce you to my sisters at once," Rebecca found herself saying, a little unnerved by the watchfulness in the lady's expression. "I—"

"You are often given responsibility for your sisters, I think," Lady Hayward said quietly. "Is that not so, Lady Rebecca?"

"It is, yes," Rebecca agreed, choosing not to hold back the truth from Lady Hayward. "My mother passed away when my youngest sister was only a babe. Since then, I have been given much of the responsibility of raising them and guiding them, although, of course, we have had governesses and the like." She tried to smile but found she could not, feeling as though she was unburdening her very soul for what would be the first time. "The three youngest are still at my father's estate, and, whilst I believe my father expects me to make a match this Season, I confess that I am not at all hopeful."

"Because you must seek out what is best for your sisters," Lady Hayward replied, clearly understanding everything Rebecca was saying without her having to express it directly. "Well, Lady Rebecca, mayhap that might change somewhat. Perhaps there is more I can do to aid you in this so that you have the opportunity yourself to find a suitable husband."

Rebecca's mouth lifted into a small, sad smile. "You are very kind, Lady Hayward," she said quietly, feeling as though she had known the lady for a good deal longer than only a few short minutes. "I will gladly welcome whatever it is you wish to offer."

Lady Haywood laughed softly, then gestured to someone or something over Rebecca's shoulder. "Perhaps we should start with the introduction of your sisters," she said as Rebecca turned around to see her sister, Lady Anna, standing only a short distance away, with something in her hands. "And then we must speak to Madame Bernadotte herself, to see what she requires of you all. No doubt, there will be measurements taken before we even consider what colors would best suit."

Rebecca felt the heavy burden of responsibility lift just a little as she turned around to lead Lady Hayward towards her sisters. This afternoon, at least, she would not be solely responsible for the gowns her sisters chose, the gowns that they would wear into society. She had Lady Hayward's experience and understanding now, even though they were only very briefly acquainted. For whatever reason, Rebecca felt as though she had found a caring and concerned individual whose eagerness to help came from a place of true kindness, and for that, she found herself increasingly grateful.

"Anna," she said, seeing her other sister standing a short distance away. "And Selina, might you join us for a moment?" Waiting until both had joined them, Rebecca turned to Lady Hayward. "Lady Hayward, might I present my two sisters." She gestured to the first. "This is Lady Anna, and next to her, Lady Selina."

Lady Hayward curtsied. "I am glad to make your acquaintance."

"And this is Lady Hayward," Rebecca told her sisters, who were both looking at her with a mixture of confusion and interest. "Father has returned to the townhouse and has left Lady Hayward to assist us in choosing our gowns. We will return with her once we are finished here."

Her sisters' eyes widened in evident surprise, but Anna was the first one to speak, excited tones pouring from her mouth as she engaged Lady Hayward in conversation almost at once. She spoke about colors and gloves and ribbons, begging Lady Hayward to join her so that she might show her what she had been considering. Rebecca smiled to herself, thinking that it was very much like Anna to be so eager, whilst Selina, as she expected, stayed back just a little, watching carefully but having none of the enthusiasm of her twin sister.

"You have only just met Lady Hayward, then?" Lady Selina asked as Rebecca nodded. "And Father is quite contented to allow her to help us?"

"*More* than willing, I should say," Rebecca replied

with a sudden smile. "In fact, I do not think he was hesitant for barely a moment! The opportunity to return to the townhouse and to remove himself from supervising the choosing of gowns was one he could not simply ignore." She chuckled, and, finally, Lady Selina smiled. "I think we may have found an ally in Lady Hayward, Selina." A jolt of happiness ran through her frame, and Rebecca allowed herself to sigh with contentment. "Perhaps this Season will not be as difficult as I feared after all."

CHAPTER TWO

"I do hope there will be no tardiness this evening!"

Rebecca sat up straight in her chair as her father came striding into the room, only to stop dead as he caught sight of not one but three of his daughters sitting quietly together, waiting for him to join them. He cleared his throat and nodded at them, muttering something under his breath that Rebecca could not quite make out.

Rebecca felt delighted with his reaction, but, of course, hid it well. It would not do to have her father irritated just before they left the house for what would be their very first foray into society.

"Now that you have been presented," the Duke said, coming to stand in front of the small fire that burned in the grate, keeping the evening's chill away from the large room, "it is time to enter society. You are, however, to be on your guard."

Rebecca frowned. "If you are to suggest, Father, that we do not know what is expected of us in terms of behavior, then—"

"That is not at all what I am suggesting, Rebecca, and kindly do not interrupt," the duke said firmly, his eyes fixing to hers as she quelled her frustration. "I am well aware that my daughters know what is proper and what is improper. I fully expect this evening to go very well, indeed. What I am to say, however, is that you all must be careful of those you are introduced to. Some will be eager for your acquaintance, of course, which will be rather flattering." His lips thinned, giving Rebecca the impression that he had been through an experience that had not pleased him. "It will be a matter of wisdom and consideration to know whether such people are eager for your acquaintance out of an eagerness to become known to you, or if they seek it out for their own gain."

Rebecca's heart began to grow heavy. She had been looking forward to this evening, especially with the promise of Lady Hayward being present also. The purchasing of their gowns had gone very well indeed and, whilst Rebecca did not know what Lady Hayward and her father had discussed thereafter, she felt quite certain that the duke would be very contented indeed with their acquaintance continuing. Now, however, she feared that her father would expect her to ensure that her sisters were acquainted only with those that were of excellent character and had no underlying motives—although quite how she was meant to decipher such a thing, Rebecca had very little idea.

"Therefore, you must be on your guard," the duke said firmly. "If, for any reason, a gentleman is eager to further his acquaintance with you, you shall give his name to me, and I shall do some investigation into his situation before any further interaction takes place."

"Yes, Father," the three young ladies murmured together, with Rebecca's heart sinking all the lower. She would never be able to find a suitable match, not when her father's demands were so stringent. What if she found someone she considered appropriate, only for her father to refuse on some small matter? She knew that the duke expected his daughters to marry well, to gentlemen of excellent title, of good family, and of substantial wealth. Now, it seemed, she had to find such a gentleman but would also be required to ensure that his character was without fault and his motivations quite pure. It felt like a near-impossible task.

The duke cleared his throat, his hands still clasped tightly behind his back, and Rebecca forced herself to give him her full attention and did not linger on any further thoughts at present.

"There is another matter that I wish to inform you of," the duke continued as Rebecca let out a long, slow breath, a little frustrated that there appeared to be even more the duke required of them. "It is to do with Lady Hayward."

Rebecca's heart dropped to the floor. No doubt, then, the duke had found something disparaging about the lady and had decided that she was not a suitable acquaintance for his daughters. Perhaps that was what had been discussed yesterday afternoon when they had returned from Madame Bernadotte's. Perhaps Lady Hayward had been thanked by the duke but asked to remove herself from their acquaintance. It was quite feasible, given all that the duke expected, and yet Rebecca felt sorrowful, having thought very highly of Lady Hayward.

"As you know, Lady Hayward is a kind and willing lady who has very little to occupy her at present," the duke began, his voice rolling through the room. "I was grateful to her for her assistance yesterday, and I am sure that, given how highly you all spoke of her, you were grateful for her company also."

"We were, Father," Lady Anna replied quietly. "I believe we all thought very highly of her."

"Good." The duke paused for a moment and, much to Rebecca's astonishment, began to smile. What was it he was going to reveal? She was no longer as certain as she had been about her father's intentions, praying that he would not ask them to separate from the lady entirely.

"Lady Hayward has a son. Three, in fact," the duke continued, now looking pleased with himself. "There are a few issues concerning the late Lord Hayward's will, and, in addition, I believe the new Lord Hayward is struggling just a little with all that has been placed upon his shoulders." He shrugged. "It is understandable when one takes the title to be a little overwhelmed, but there are certain matters that make things a good deal more difficult for Lord Hayward. Therefore, having discussed the matter at length with Lady Hayward, she and I have come to a mutually agreed arrangement."

A flurry of either fear or excitement—for Rebecca could not tell which—ran down her spine as she listened intently, wondering what it could be that had been agreed upon. It was not like her father to go about such things in this way, for he did not like to ask anyone for their help or assistance in anything, being quite determined to do it without interference. And yet, in this case, it appeared as though this was precisely what he had done.

"I have no interest in attending balls, in encouraging matches and in chaperoning waltzes and the like," the duke said with a wave of his hand and a sigh of exasperation. "Lady Hayward has no real interest in business matters, although, of course, she wishes to aid her son in any way she can. Therefore, we have both agreed to be of assistance to the other."

Silence filled the room for a few minutes as the three ladies looked at their father expectantly, clearly ready for him to say more, but it seemed as though the duke was finished with his explanations. With a shrug, he turned and gestured to the door. "Let us hurry now. She will be waiting."

Rebecca did not move from her chair. "What do you mean, Father?" she asked as Lady Anna and Lady Selina watched the duke with curiosity. "Lady Hayward is to assist you? In what way?"

"By chaperoning you, of course," he said, a slight flicker crossing his brow as though he had expected them all to understand what he meant without difficulty. "She will do what I do not wish to and will guide you through society and make certain that any gentlemen who wish to acquaint themselves a little more with you are entirely suitable."

. . .

What a gift for Lady Rebecca! She now has the lovely Lady Hayward to assist her with her debut into the *ton* and help her find a husband. To find out what happens next, please check out **Mistaken for a Rake** on the Kindle store! Mistaken for a Rake